The Invisible Web

The Invisible Web

by
Clarence Hester

DORRANCE PUBLISHING CO., INC.
PITTSBURGH, PENNSYLVANIA 15222

The contents of this work including, but not limited to, the accuracy of events, people, and places, depicted; opinions expressed; permission to use previously published materials included; and any advice given or actions advocated are solely the responsibility or the author, who assumes all liability for said work and indemnifies the publisher against any claims stemming from publication of the work.

All Rights Reserved
Copyright © 2006 by Clarence Hester
No part of this book may be reproduced or transmitted in any form or by any means, electronic or mechanical, including photocopying, recording, or by any information storage and retrieval system without permission in writing from the publisher.

ISBN-10: 0-8059-7018-5
ISBN-13: 978-0-8059-7018-0
Printed in the United States of America

First Printing

For information or to order additional books, please write:
Dorrance Publishing Co., Inc.
701 Smithfield Street
Third Floor
Pittsburgh, Pennsylvania 15222
U.S.A.
1-800-788-7654
Or visit our website and online catalogue at www.dorrancebookstore.com

Dedication

This book is dedicated to my mother.

Foreword

Although this literary work is considered fiction, it is based on actual events. The author expertly brings to life the contrasting worlds of the wealthy to middle-class white Americans to that of poor and miseducated blacks of the inner cities across the United States.

Most black men become conscious of their actual plight courtesy of the country's overcrowded penal system. History reveals one of the greatest examples of this fact to be Malcolm X, who self-educated himself while in prison and went on to becomeone of our most prolific philosophers, thinkers, and opposers of injustice. Basically, only during incarceration do most black men have time to actually analyze his situation and that of his people. It is then that he begins to think for himself and to research history, which sparks his brain and leads to the quest to discover how things became such as they are. Unfortunately, after finding out the truth while in prison, the individual is forced back into his former surroundings upon release, where survival is the only objective. Many people do not realize that in the ghettoes and inner cities, where most blacks in this country live, car-jackings, robberies, and murders are accepted as a fact of life. White Americans could hardly fathom existing in a place where gunshots and sirens are constantly heard nearby; whereas their black counterparts view witnessing a homicide or drug deal as if it were as insignificant as swatting a fly. The criminal justice system has basically dealt with the situation much in the same way as the majority of the unenlightened society, and that is by concentrating and placing the blame on the perpetrator of the offense rather than even attempting to uncover the circumstances that produced this irrational behavior.

Perhaps it is much easier to turn a blind eye to the problem and the causes thereof than to admit the obvious—that being either the system was designed to produce these results or that it has failed to prevent or correct them.

It would be wise to read this book studiously; whereas it goes to the very root of the problems that plague black people of this country. Through the life of

Jamal, a black excon who is released from prison back to his old neighborhood, we learn a valuable lesson of the aforementioned facts. Determined to educate and uplift his race, Jamal is thrown back into the lion's den of the ghetto and receives a rude awakening when he is slapped right in the face with the reality of the deterioration of an already dreadful situation. Regardless of the opposition, Jamal still finds time to enlighten a well-to-do white woman by exposing her to the verity of conditions in which poor blacks live.

She is shocked by the blacks' acceptance of extreme poverty as well as their propensity to commit violent acts on one another at any moment. Even more shocking is that they seemingly have become immune to a bullet or spending decades behinds bars, This story opens the eyes of the reader, whether black or white, to this gloomy state of affairs—and whether society will wait until this brutality is inflicted upon the privileged class of white Americans before looking for solutions,

—Don Hardy

To My Road Dog, on Lock Down

Even though you're not with us, your presence is still felt like the ruins of a hurricane. And though you may be an enemy to the state, to us, the brothers in the hood, you are a hero. You ran the risk by taking from the rich, the bloodsuckers of the poor, in order to spread a little joy among the not-so-fortunate.

You are honored and respected among those in the hood who have not yet tasted the triumphs of robbing the system that has so methodically kept us down for centuries.

You rose up cold and calculated and took on the system head on by the only means you understood, and now they want you to pay with your life thrown back into their hands for maximum control, but they fail to understand that you are a soldier captured in a battle for survival which can only contain your physical composition but never your state of mind.

I can truly say you have freed yourself from them forever; you cannot be fooled or deceived by the illusions projected to society that keep most people wielded within their views.

I watched and observed you half of my life and you never conformed to their doctrines; you always thought for yourself, which cost you years of incarceration, but you never cried or complained; you just seemed to get stronger; you always held your end down, took your own weight and the weight of some of the weaker.

And what I admire about you most, is that they could never break you or cause you to lose your humanity.

You have always helped the less fortunate; came to the rescue of the disadvantaged and never asked for anything in return;

I've never seen you in church, but your deeds reflect a heart of an angel;

I've never seen you pray. But you have forgiven and forgotten when dealing with your brotherman, a divine attribute of the righteous.

And no matter what they call you or say about you. . . . Remember you always have our vote. . . .

Peace,
The Hood

ACKNOWLEDGEMENTS

Working under adverse conditions usually makes the job twice as hard as it really is. However, through serious dedication, determination and reliability, I was able to weave my way through obstacles and complete this book.

My main source of reliability rested upon my mother, who provided financial and spiritual support for the creation of this work. My next source came from my business associate, Mr. Jackie McKubbin, who put his fingers to work, typed the manuscript, and also helped in other areas as well. I would also like to give recognition to Mr. Latimas Wingate, a.k.a. "T. Byrd," a special friend of mine who provided me with a character name and gave me his assessment of the book before going into print. And a special thanks to Benny Paul, a.k.a. "Stepper," who critically assessed the book in its early stages, which made the difference in its outcome.

Chapter 1

As the prison gates slammed behind him, Jamal took a deep breath and uttered, "Free at last."

It had been a long hard, thirteen years with a large portion of it spent in solitary confinement due to his failure to conform and adjust to the prison's dictates. He had done the max on his time; there was no one to report to, he was totally on his own.

He finally reached the little depot where the prisoners who were being released either waited on someone to come pick them up or a cab to take them to the bus station.

The guard at the depot waved him past, so he set his belongings down and stretched out on the bench that sat on the side of the depot. He began to sort out his thoughts on what he would do once he hit the city. Detroit was a rough town when it came to survival, even with its vast car industry. It has one of the highest rates of unemployment in the nation.

Serious cutbacks in government funding for welfare and other social programs caused an increase in hunger and homelessness, sinking to the level of human rights violations, considering this country's mass abundance of wealth; again Detroit was right at the top of the list of government cutbacks.

Jamal, being a very socially and political conscious person, was acutely aware of the new crisis he now faced as he approached the so-called free world, which he understood to be free for some, hell for others. Even though it's a wonderful feeling being free from the clutches of the prison industrial complex, he was now haunted by the new dilemma of falling in the hands of the socioeconomic conditions that sent him there in the first place. It was a very frightening feeling that could not be realized unless placed in that predicament. He certainly didn't want to commit a crime (as society would term it) and return to prison, but his chances of gaining meaningful employment in the highly skilled labor force was a million to one.

Yet, in spite of all the adversity he faced, Jamal was determined to slip through the loophole that trapped so many like himself into hell's triangle—**THE INVISI-BLE WEB,** plagued by death, life imprisonment, or the soup line....

While caught in deep thought, he never noticed the orange-white cab that pulled up to the depot until the horn blew. His head jerked up, and it dawned on him that this was his transportation to the bus station, away from that awful stench of prison. He walked up to the cab, gave his last look at the prison (in total defiance), and hopped in. The driver was an older Chinese fellow with small-framed glasses who asked, "You go bus stop?"

Jamal answered, "Yeah, yeah." And the cab spun off. Upon arriving at the bus stop, Jamal jumped out, gave the driver a twenty-dollar bill, and said, "Keep the change."

"You good man," the driver said and added, "thank you, have nice day." And the cab spun off again.

As he entered the bus terminal, he noticed a few people sitting around who looked bored; he could just about tell from that look that they were waiting for a bus and had been there awhile. He walked up to the ticket window and received his scheduled ticket for Detroit. When he turned around he felt as though everyone in the terminal was watching him. The first thing that came to mind was, *It must be these damn clothes*, he thought, *way out of style. I knew I should have gotten my own clothes sent up to me instead of this prison clown suit.*

The last thing he wanted to do was draw attention to himself fresh out of the joint. Then he thought, *Maybe it's me, I've been gone over a decade; I'm probably so out of tune with everything I can't help but stand out—or is this just my imagination?*

He wrestled, then he told himself, *Man pull yourself together. This ain't nothing to be tripping about; it's too small. You got a heavy task that awaits you out here.* So he decided to take a seat and just chill out.

While sitting there reading a newspaper he happened to notice the young lady who walked through the door. She was young, early twenties at the most, very attractive with an air of sophistication, yet appeared to be more of the down-to-earth type. She had long black hair tied in a ponytail, a rich complexion, dark eyes, and a radiant smile that seemed to light up the whole building. She had natural beauty along with a well-proportioned body—everything a man dreamed of, especially coming out of prison. But there was that one thing that almost always stood in the way, that barrier: She was white, he's black, yet he thought, *Hadn't things changed over the years? Yeah probably so, but not when it came to that. This is a racist society we live in where everything you do is determined by the color of your skin. That has never changed and probably never will.*

However, what had happened over the course of time was that appearances had changed. Where on the surface it appeared that interracial association and affiliation was socially accepted, deep down inside it was regarded as a reproach to many people.

From his experience of dealing with white people he learned to never initiate any interaction with them, more as a protective policy that would keep him from winding up in an embarrassing situation. On the other hand, if the action was brought to him he would feel justified upon any reaction.

Just as he was completing his thoughts on the subject the young lady came over and sat down beside him. He thought to himself, *Damn, why did she have to come over here?* It made him feel uncomfortable. She even looked lovelier up close than when she walked through the door, he felt. Then that did it; she had to break the silence, as he had feared.

"Excuse me," she said, "you wouldn't happen to have another newspaper or something else to read, would you? I'm bored," she added, "the bus isn't due for another hour and a half."

"You can read this one if you like. I have books and magazines in my belongings," Jamal offered.

"That sounds even better. What type of books do you have?"

"History, philosophy, economics, and some political stuff."

"That sounds interesting. What are you majoring in?" she asked him.

"Majoring in?" he had to think a second; *What the hell is she talking about?* Then he then he thought, *Oh yeah, that college stuff.* "I hate to disappoint you, but I never attended college a day in my life."

"Oh that's okay. I just have a habit of thinking that everyone I see with books is in school."

"You must be busting the college thing yourself?" She looked puzzled. Jamal noticed and rephrased the question. "I mean, you must attend yourself?"

"Yes I just finished my sophomore year and should get my B.A. next year."

Now he looked puzzled, but she didn't notice. They were definitely from two different worlds but struggling to comprehend one another.

Jamal reached into his belongings and handed her a couple of books he had gotten out. "Here, you want to check these out?"

"Oh thank you," she replied, reaching for them.

He could sense that she was very intellectual in her approach to knowledge. He himself was well read and self-educated more so than through the educational system.

As she skimmed through the pages of the books he could see her eyebrows raise, an indication that she hadn't expected this type of literature to come from him.

"Are you working on some type of project?"

"Not really, why you ask that?"

"Well that's some pretty heavy stuff you're toying with. You have to be above average in literary comprehension to absorb that."

He knew what she was implying, that this wasn't the type of level the common street dude (ghetto) was on.

"Really, I just developed an early thirst for knowledge that introduced me to a new world of inquiry."

"What led you in that direction?" she asked.

Boy, she's getting deep now, he thought. *There's no way I'll be able to get around telling her I've been to prison.*

"Well, the many nights spent within the gloom of darkness, wondering where my life was headed or if I was to have a life at all, brought on some intellectual challenges for me."

"Oh I get the picture now. It was prison that changed your life around."

"You got part of it right: it was prison, but I wouldn't go as far as to say it changed my life around."

"Why do you say that?" she asked.

"Because the conditions that surround my life are the same, and at the present my life is governed by those conditions. There's been no transformation in my life, only in my approach to life."

"You certainly don't fit the stigma attached to prison."

"May I ask how that stigma is characterized?"

"Commonly most people think of the prisoner as brutal, violent, aggressive, short on the use of brains, and not too well mannered."

"Well I'll be damned; I never knew we were thought of like that," Jamal stated.

"Undoubtedly you've proven that to be ludicrous. By the way, I never got your name," she said.

"Oh yeah, my name is Jamal."

"It is certainly interesting meeting you, Jamal; my name is Cathy."

Boy, she certainly is cordial, he thought to himself.

"The pleasure is all mine," he said.

"How long were you in prison?" she asked.

"Thirteen years."

"Thirteen years!" she said in amazement.

"Yeah, thirteen big ones."

"What did you do, murder someone?"

Damn! That's a helluva question to ask somebody, he said to himself. He really didn't want to respond, but he had allowed himself to be set up for it.

"Naw, it wasn't a murder; it was a robbery and an off-duty policeman was shot after he shot one of the robbers. They made a big deal out of it and thought we should be put away for a long while."

"How old were you then?"

Damn, she must be writing a book, he said to himself. "Seventeen."

"You really haven't had a chance to live your adult life then, have you?"

"Not really," he said and added, "but it's no big thing. I wasn't doing much with my life anyway."

"Were you ever locked up before then?"

"Yeah, I went to the training school when I was thirteen and stayed until I was fifteen."

"Okay, now I understand your answer of not doing much with your life; over half of it has been wasted behind bars."

No kidding, he thought, *what the hell is she, a psych or somebody? The hell with all this, I am going to ask the questions now.* "So where are you headed?" he asked curiously.

"Detroit, I'm out of school for the summer."

"Detroit!" he said rather shocked.

"Well actually I live right outside of Detroit: Sterling Heights, as a matter of fact, but I'll have to take the bus to Detroit first."

Damn, he thought, *just my luck. She'll probably follow me now, thinking we're acquainted and can kick it.* It wasn't bad having her around, as she was attractive and quite intelligent, he reasoned, but it would draw a lot of attention—something he really didn't want. As he was thinking about it, it was being announced over the loudspeaker: "Destination; Detroit: bus leaves in five minutes. Please board now!"

"Are you ready for a nice long ride?" she asked Jamal.

"Yeah, I guess so. You want me to help you with your bags?"

"Please," she said.

It was obvious now that they would be making the trip together; she probably found him interesting enough to keep from being bored the whole trip. *Oh well, what the hell*, he thought. *It couldn't hurt anything.*

Once they boarded the bus she guided him to a seat and asked, "Do you want the inside or outside?"

"I'll take the outside. I'm going to have to stretch my legs a lot."

After all, he was rather tall, about six feet, and she was an average size for a woman, five-six or five-seven at the most.

After he finished putting their things up on the rack, he sat down, adjusted the seat, and kicked back. She was sitting up looking out of the window. He had come to the conclusion that they wouldn't get much sleep, as he could detect her mood for adventure.

"Why did you look so shocked when I said I was going to Detroit?" she asked him.

"Because you didn't fit the stigma," he said, anxious to get back at her.

"Oh! Because I'm white," she stated.

"Not really, because there are whites living in the city of Detroit, but they are rejects from mainstream society whom they refer to as poor white trash."

"I've heard that term used but never grasped its full significance."

"Of course not. They don't teach that in school, you feel me?"

"Feel you!" she repeated.

"I mean do you feel what I'm trying to get across to you?" he said, frustrated at himself for forgetting their cultural difference.

"Oh I get it, she said." You can't learn everything in school."

"Exactly," he said firmly.

"So from my appearance I would look out of place in Detroit, being white."

"In most areas yeah, except the business district areas in downtown."

"Okay, I'm getting the picture now. The whites with money and good jobs are common in the business district."

"True," he added, "and most of these whites live in the suburbs and only show up for business purposes."

"That certainly is amazing when you think about it," she stated.

"Not really. It's no different than during the time of slavery, as the slave master never came down to the slaves' quarters to mingle with the slaves; he only came to the fields to count how many bales of cotton were picked."

"Can you actually equate that with the current situation?" she stated more than asked.

"It all boils down to the same thing; capital gain supersedes social equality in the eyes and interests of America."

Cathy was becoming overwhelmed by his keen insight into the socioeconomic conditions that plagued the oppressed people in this country. She'd heard people speak on some of these issues but never heard it articulated with such intensity as he had done. She could feel the bitterness in his tone as if he were personally victimized by every issue he spoke on. He didn't let you off the hook, and she was somewhat intimidated by his harshness, yet captivated by his intellect.

"Now that you're out, what do you plan to do?" she asked.

"In my world there are no plans; there's nothing really to plan for. I just take it a day at a time until the system snatches me up and sends me back to prison or sends me to my grave, cut and dry."

"Well since you know that, why not do what you can to avoid it?"

"In my case it's just a matter of time; there's no avoiding it. The same as if someone has a contract out on your life—you can run, but you can't hide. I'm a marked man; the power structure has a contract out on all aggressive black males who refuse to accept a subservient role in this society. When you see many of these broke-down skinning-and-grinning-before-the-white-man Negroes, they are not themselves; they are acting out the role that this society has picked for them. They are controlled to never speak out or act against the injustices their people encounter on a daily basis. That's part of their role, bought and paid for, for an extra crumb or two."

That was a very powerful statement, and she went over it again in her mind. She was now beginning to understand that here was an angry individual who had lost all faith in the system and had no hope for the future, but at the same time she could sense a powerful inner strength in him. *He must have a strong belief in something*, she surmised, so she asked, "Do you believe in God?"

This was a heated subject that he'd learned to stay away from, especially in prison with all of the religious fanatics floating around the compound, but he would make an exception in her case since she inquired of him.

"Not in the traditional sense," he answered then added, "where the belief in God is a separate entity from man/woman. To me God is the highest extent of the human mind, the supreme intelligence, the highest state of consciousness. He/she cannot be found outside of self. When referred to as the supreme being, one must understand the being is existence, and supreme is the highest form of that existence, combined together they equal the highest existence of the human stage; to me there can be no other existence."

This really blew her mind; she had never in her life encountered such a belief or ran into anyone who represented such a belief.

"That is quite some belief," she stated. "Is that from a particular school of thought, or is that your own analysis?"

Jamal took his time to answer that. "I would say from an assortment of study and investigation; I've come to draw my own conclusions."

"So am I correct to assume you embrace no religion?" she asked with anticipation.

"You are so correct," he said and added, "religion to me is nothing but a social philosophy created by man as a guide to live by; it has nothing to do with the concept of God."

"Why do you refer to God as a concept?"

"Because that's all it is. It's just a matter of how you believe or who you believe it to be, but it all boils down to a matter of belief, nothing concrete to establish it," he concluded with confidence.

Then all of a sudden silence fell upon them. She lay back to absorb a lot of the things he had spoken on, especially the latter. Though her family was of the Christian faith, she was not a staunch believer and seldom went to church, as she was not convinced of its accuracy in the way it was being taught.

Jamal was also in deep thought, wondering if he had been too harsh with her by expressing such offset views that weren't readily accepted by most, as they tend to upset the established order of things, but they were his views and he would air them whenever the occasion arose.

Cathy had really grown to admire this man in the short time she had known him and wondered what would become of his life. She had guessed his age to be about thirty, single, no children, with more than half of his life spent behind bars.

Would he be able to get a job? Very unlikely, she thought, with already two strikes against him (African-American male/ex-convict). How would he survive? More than likely he was going back to a violent, crime-ridden, drug-infested neighborhood, with no means of transportation, no cash available to sustain his livelihood, well informed in the ways of the world, and extremely possessed with self pride. Frightening when you think about it. *My God! He was right: a sure ticket back to prison or an early pass to the grave for a man in his shoes.*

She had become extremely sensitive to his plight; she had to help in some way, she thought. But what would she do? Help him find a job? That was no solution, but it was certainly a start. However, she must be cautious, as she knew nothing of the man personally other than what he told her. He could be dangerous; after all, he did go to prison for a violent crime, but somehow he seemed to be a very warm and caring person on the inside and she trusted him.

"We should be getting pretty close to Detroit now," she seemed to be thinking out loud.

"Yeah, it shouldn't be long now," he responded.

"Jamal, I know you're not one for plans, but it's rough out here, especially for a person coming home from prison."

Oh here we go with the ole symphony for the downtrodden, Jamal thought to himself.

"I feel the least I can do is help you find a decent job where you can sustain yourself without having to compromise your principles."

"And what may I offer you as an act of good faith?" he said.

"You can guide me to the accessing of worldly knowledge such as you have obtained."

"You got a deal," Jamal said and added, "fair exchange is no robbery."

"Here's my address and phone number where I can be contacted," she said, handing him a slip of paper.

"I don't know if that is such a good idea in the eyes of Sterling Heights. I'd feel better if you contact me and we meet on neutral ground."

"Oh dear me, you've been locked up too long, but if it makes you feel more comfortable, we'll do that."

"Here you go; this is my hook-up. Just ask for me; if I'm not there, just leave a message."

"Wow! There's the sign; we've just reached the city limits', Cathy said with enthusiasm.

"Nothing to get excited about in this old raggedy dump."

"Oh, there's been some renovations since you've been gone."

"Not in my hood," he said.

She thought a moment; *Oh he must mean neighborhood.* She was beginning to catch on to some of the street language he used.

"Where is your neighborhood?" she asked.

"The tragedy of the Westside, Twenty-third and Buchanan. It's what they call The Pit; poor whites, hungry Mexicans, and misguided blacks, killing each other over drug money."

"A perfect setting for a guy coming home from prison, huh?" Cathy said.

"Yeah, they'll have a gun and a key of dope waiting for me as a coming-home present," Jamal said jokingly.

They both laughed but at the same time understood it to be a reality.

By now the bus was pulling into the terminal. When the bus stopped, Jamal picked up her baggage and carried them into the station, and she carried his few belongings. He set the baggage down and shook her hand and said, "Well, this is it, Cathy—at least for now."

"I enjoyed our little time together; it's been one heck of an experience for me."

"Yeah, me too," he said walking off.

Chapter 2

Jamal walked through the bus station; nothing much had changed since he'd been gone, only the people. Everyone seemed to be in a frantic rush, and people's attitudes were cold toward one another. Most of the young people walked around in groups with looks on their faces as if they had an attitude at the whole world. He decided to go outside and hail a cab and get on home before it got too late; it was already about 8:30 in the evening.

He stepped out on the curb to flag a cab.

"Yo! Taxi! Taxi!" He hollered at the top of his voice, but none seemed to hear him as they sped by. The cabs were picking up people everywhere as the bus terminal was extremely crowed. This was the time of year people traveled extensively; school would soon be closing for the summer, and people were taking their vacations. Detroit was getting ready for the Grand Prix race car events, and the N.A.A.C.P. were having their convention; a lot was going on in the city of Detroit at this time.

Jamal stepped into the street. "Yo! Taxi! Right here!"

One pulled up along side of him, and he jumped in. "Where to my man?" the driver said.

"Twenty-third and Buchanan," Jamal told the cab driver as the cab was moving.

The driver slammed the brakes and said, "Aw naw, my man, I don't go up in there at night; it's a war zone, sorry."

As Jamal got out of the cab, he thought to himself, *He's probably just scared.* He tried another cab.

"Yo! Yo! Taxi!"

One pulled up alongside of him, and he hopped in. The driver was Mexican. "Where to, amigo?"

"Twenty-third and Buchanan,"

"Man, you loco? That's The Pit. It's too dark; no street lights."

"Why is that?" Jamal asked.

"All them shot out. Nobody goes in there at night; it's suicide. I can take you to Michigan Ave; that's far as I go."

"That's all right, I'll chill, thanks."

After he got out of that cab, he went back inside the bus station. He couldn't understand why everybody was so leery about going into his neighborhood at night; had it gotten that crazy out there? Maybe so. He would have to call his sister now to see if he could get her to come pick him up. He went to a pay phone to call Yolanda, his sister. The phone rang, and his nephew, Poochi, who was six years old, picked up the receiver. "Yeah, who is it?"

"It's Jamal."

"Jamal!" He sounded a little confused. "I thought you was supposed to be coming home today."

"I am home, fool; I'm at the bus Station. Is your mama there?"

"Yeah she here."

"Let me talk to her."

"Okay, hold on. . . . Yo Red! Tell Mama Jamal is on the phone."

"Mama! Jamal on the phone."

Yolanda was thirty-three years old and already had four kids, ages six months to sixteen, but she still looked young healthy, a very pretty woman by most standards.

"Hello," she said as she grabbed the phone from her son.

"Yo, what's up?" Jamal greeted her.

"Where you at?" she asked.

"I'm at the bus station; can you come pick me up?"

"That's going to be a problem," she said.

"Why is that?"

"There ain't no car here right now."

"Where's it at?" Jamal asked suspiciously.

"Raymond's got it riding around somewhere."

"Damn, you let that boy get the car? He ain't old enough for that."

"He is now; he's got his license."

"What am I supposed to do now?"

"You're going to have to chill until he shows up. I'm sure there's no cab coming out here after dark."

"Yeah, I already tried that."

"Just keep calling back, and whenever he shows up I'll make sure somebody comes and picks you up."

"Yeah awright," he said and hung up.

There wasn't much to do, so he went into the bar that was inside the bus station to have a drink. The bar was relatively crowded, a lot of traffic in and out; others were sitting around talking, probably waiting for their bus or ride home just as he was. He spotted a booth in the corner where someone had just gotten up and left, and he immediately grabbed it before someone else did, The barmaid saw him take a seat at the booth and came over and asked. "What'll you have, sugar?"

She was the ideal bar maid: superb figure, pretty face, and magnificent personality.

"Gin and lime on the rocks," he said.

She came back with his drink, a beautiful smile on her face. "Anything else?" She asked.

"No thanks," he said. He tipped her and winked at the same time. She winked back, turned on her heels, and left. He watched her as she left, then whispered, "Not bad."

After he washed her from his mind he sipped his drink and began to sort out his thoughts. He knew definitely now that the first thing he needed to get was a gun—just plain survival, he rationalized, too many fools running around with them trying to act tough. But the last thing he wanted to happen was to have to go back to prison for putting one of them fools in the ground; he would have to be extra cautious in avoiding that type of situation.

His mind suddenly switched to Cathy. Would he really take her up on that offer? He didn't really want to, but he really couldn't see anybody hiring him. He had no employment record; they'd want to know what the hell he'd been doing for the past thirteen years. If he told them he'd been in prison and for what, he was sure not to get hired. He just may have to take her up on that job offer; after all, things were just not in his favor.

As he snapped out of his thoughts he happened to look up and see a tall thin light-skinned fellow with a beak nose and long drooping mustache step through the door looking for someone, He looked just like a dude he knew named Byrd. It was Byrd, and he hollered, "Yo Byrd!"

Byrd looked his way and threw his hands up and said. "Aw man! Jamal! What's up, dog?"

Everyone in the bar seemed to look at Byrd going over to the booth to join Jamal. Byrd had the real distinct look of a killer, which he was. He had done seven years on his last bid in the joint: notorious gunman from the north end, noted for taking down some pretty big scores and called in to handle some heavy assignments.

Jamal and he greeted each other with the gangster's hug and slid into the booth to kick it a minute.

"Damn baby, when you get out?" Byrd asked.

"I'm fresh out. I ain't been to the crib yet."

"Damn man, you looking good. Took care of yourself, huh?"

"Yeah you know it. I left you up north, didn't I?" he said to Byrd.

"Yeah, eighty-nine."

"So what you been up to, Byrd?"

"Man, you know me, I sting good and lay back for a minute. Keeps me out of the madness."

"Well I'm glad I ran across you."

"Yeah what's up, you need some dough?"

"I ain't worried about that, I need a heater."

"Oh, you trying to get busy already?"

"Naw naw, it's just for personal use, 'cause I see thing have changed."

"Yeah it's kind of whack out here, but yo, it ain't no problem. I'll get you hooked up tomorrow."

"Yeah. I appreciate it."

"You on parole?" Byrd asked.

"Naw, I maxed out."

"Oh yeah, you in good shape. You want me to line something up for you?"

"Naw not right now. I'm going to chill for a minute. I'll let you know when I'm ready."

"Yeah, well you know, just holler."

The barmaid came to the booth to ask Byrd if he wanted anything to drink, he declined, as he didn't like to hang in one spot too long.

"Yo, you ready to raise?" Byrd said.

"Yeah let's get out of here."

"I was supposed to meet somebody at the bus terminal; I guess I missed them," Byrd said and added, "Anyway we can go to my ride and I'll give you a lift to the crib."

"Let me call Yolanda first and let her know I got a ride. She was coming to pick me up when the car came back."

Byrd had forgotten all about Jamal's sister Yolanda. They were around the same age; Byrd was thirty-two. He hadn't seen her in awhile, as she didn't hang out, having all those kids, but he always remembered her as a nice catch for somebody.

Jamal had just finished dialing the number and someone picked it up and hollered, "Hello!"

"Hello, who is this?"

Red, who you want?" his niece asked him.

"Call your mama to the phone. It's Jamal."

"Mama! Jamal on the phone."

"Oh I'm sorry, Jamal, I almost forgot."

"Forgot? What, you been drinking or something?"

"Uuh uh, Kisha came by and started running her mouth and took my mind off everything."

"Well don't trip; I got a ride right now anyway."

"Who?" she asked.

"Byrd."

"*Byrd!* Oh my God, you starting off on the wrong foot already."

"No I ain't; he's just giving me a lift."

"Yeah I'll bet."

"I'll be there in a few, bye," he said as he hung up.

Yolanda and Jamal had always been close, and even though most of her life she had always seemed to be going to visit him at some place of incarceration, she never abandoned him. She knew Byrd more by reputation, though she had run across him on a couple of occasions when they were younger. But it seemed as though every time she heard his name mentioned it was always associated with violence, and he was the last person she felt that Jamal needed to be with, just getting out of prison.

Byrd kept a nice car, but nothing too lavish so as not to draw attention, for he had no visible means of support, either legal or illegal.

Jamal and Byrd reached the Honda that Byrd owned. As they got into the car, Byrd said. "I can get you a .45 automatic; is that straight?"

"Oh yeah, that'll work."

"Man, whatever you do, don't let any of these jokers trick you off into the dope game."

"Why is that?" Jamal asked curiously just to see what the reason was.

"Because the only one's that survive are those that broke bad. They all wind up giving each other up in the end; that's why I rob them suckers and put 'em to rest. Ain't no loyalty in that game; cash rules. They're crossing each other left and right," Byrd gave his analysis.

"Well you know I ain't on that page anyway," Jamal told him.

"You still on that revolutionary stuff?" Byrd said with amazement.

"Yeah, if I decide to go, I'll get mine from the establishment."

"Yeah I heard ya," Byrd said, "but I ain't messing with them white folks' shit no more if I can help I; they trying to put a brother away for good."

"Yeah, I been thinking, I ain't really trying to do nothing. I might get a job and slow it down a little bit; I've been putting too much time in up state."

"Yeah, I feel ya," Byrd said.

"Yo, stop at the party store on Michigan Avenue. I'm going to play a lottery ticket; I feel it. You know what they say about beginner's luck."

Byrd pulled into the parking lot of a party store owned by Arabs. Most of the party stores and grocery stores were Arab owned, as an influx of Arabs had flooded the Detroit area in the past five to ten years, using their wealth to buy out most of the black-owned businesses. Jamal hopped out and went inside; when he came back to the car he had a look of disgust on his face and was sort of mumbling to himself when he climbed in, but it was loud enough for Byrd to hear him. "Goddamn Arabs trying to take over our communities."

"Yeah, black folks out here are weak and stupid. They let them Arabs come in and offer them double the price of what they making, and they sell the business to them, and the Arab calls his whole family over, and they own that store for generations," Byrd commented.

"Yeah, I know that black people are stupid, but those types of Arabs are sell-outs to the Palestinian cause. Damn fools should be trying to help their brothers get their land back from them Jews instead of getting drawn into the Western culture," Jamal explained.

As Byrd pulled out of the parking lot Jamal noticed Byrd pull out his gun from under the seat.

"Damn, what's up, Byrd? You got beef down, this way?"

"Naw, but you got a lot of jack boys in this hood. You got to stay ready with finger on the trigger, you know what I'm saying?"

"Yeah I feel ya," Jamal said.

They rode down the dark street. There were no street lights working, nobody was on the streets, all too quiet. All you could hear were the crickets. They had no doubt entering The Pit it was indeed frightening; it was as if you were entering a ghost town.

"Don't look like you have to worry about no jack boys around here—or nobody else," Jamal said.

They were three blocks into The Pit when out of nowhere came the cracking sound of gunfire. They couldn't make out where it was coming from, then they saw the flashes of light coming from both sides of the street. They had no idea of who was shooting at whom. Byrd quickly mashed on the brakes, put the car in reverse, and backed up a whole block, then made a right turn onto the next street and drove all the way back up to Michigan Avenue and turned right and drove down to the boulevard. He drove very cautiously now as he did not want to run into the police or give them any reason to stop him, as not only did he have an unregistered gun, but he also was wanted for questioning in a double homicide.

"Damn, I'll mess around and get stopped on a humbug in that hood," Byrd said.

"Does that shit happen every night?" Jamal asked.

"It might happen any time over in there; them dudes always beefing."

"What do we do now?" Jamal wanted to know.

"We'll go down to the donut shop at the intersection; it's lit up down there."

"How am I going to get to the crib? I know you ain't going back down through there?"

"Call your sister and tell her to come scoop you at the donut shop, but tell her to take Martin Luther King Drive to the boulevard to Michigan Avenue after what happened. All those streets are lit up; it's longer but safer. I'll stay until she gets here to make sure you don't get left hanging."

Byrd pulled up in the parking lot of the donut shop; there were a few cars but not many. There were already a couple of people sitting at the counter when they came in, so they went to a table. They ordered coffee and donuts, and Jamal went to the phone booth in the corner and called Yolanda. The car was there, so she and her friend Kisha would come pick him up in a few minutes. He came back to the table and told Byrd that everything was straight, they'd be there in a few to get him.

Jamal was busy trying to make eye contact with the young female who was sitting at the next table along with another female when suddenly Byrd got up and eased into the phone booth as he had spotted the two policemen from the window coming toward the donut shop. Before Jamal had figured out what was going on, the two police had taken a seat at the counter. He remained calm as he didn't want to arouse any suspicion of Byrd. When he finished his coffee and donut he left a tip on the table and got up and left with the eyes of the young female following him. On his way out he noticed the phone booth was empty, Byrd had vanished like Houdini.

He stood outside, just lingering around, when a car pulled up in the parking lot; it was Yolanda and Kisha in a black Cutlass. He walked over to the car and knocked on the side window where Kisha was, and she unlocked the door and he crawled into the back seat.

"Damn, y'all don't take no chances, do you?"

"You better believe it," Kisha said; "this is carjacking territory."

"What Byrd do, leave you standing?" Yolanda asked him.

"Naw, he was here until the cops showed up."

"I think they're looking for him for those murders at the Traveler's Motel," Kisha said.

"He's just wanted for questioning," Jamal corrected her.

'Boy, you better leave that fool alone before you wind up right back where you came from," Yolanda told him.

Jamal quickly changed the subject; he didn't want to hear any more about that.

"Yo, where's the best place to shop for some clothes?" he said, asking no one in particular.

"Downtown," Kisha answered.

"Yeah, well, I need to get down there tomorrow and pick out a few outfits."

"Styles have changed somewhat since you've been gone," Yolanda told him.

"Don't matter, whatever they're wearing I'll roll with it."

"I'll take you shopping tomorrow," Yolanda told him.

"Where does everybody go at night around here?" Jamal said.

"They're either in for the night or across town, but you won't see anybody around here until tomorrow when it's light out."

By now they were pulling up in the driveway of their house. He noticed that much hadn't changed with the house except that it had been painted and more trees had grown in the back yard. It was the house he had grown up in with four other children, he being the youngest. His father had been killed during the riots by police when he was just a baby. His mother had struggled to raise all five of them but years later had gotten a large sum of money from a settlement in a suit filed for the wrongful death of her husband. She moved out of the house and to the suburbs by the time Yolanda was grown enough to take over the house, which was already paid for. Her other children had moved out west, all except Jamal, who by then was already in prison. Yolanda had a good-paying job as a computer operator for a business firm and had recently broken up with the kids' father, who helped support the household.

As soon as they stepped inside the house, Jamal was greeted and swarmed upon by his niece and nephew, even the little baby was smiling with joy. Everyone was there except Raymond. They all liked and respected him; he was the uncle that everyone talked about. He sat and talked with them awhile and then he told them it had been a long, hectic day for him and all he wanted to do was take a bath and go to bed. And that's exactly what he did.

Chapter 3

Jamal slept until around 10:00 A.M. the next morning, which was late for him as he was used to getting up early in the morning in prison. Even though it was a Saturday morning, everyone in the house was up by this time. As he was going to the bathroom to freshen up, Yolanda poked fun at him. "The prince has just arisen; all hail to the prince."

"Stop playing, girl," he said playfully.

"Mama, Jamal need some clothes," Wanda, her oldest daughter who was thirteen, said.

"We already know that. I'm taking him shopping today."

When he came from the bathroom, he asked, "Anybody call for me?"

"Not yet, you expecting someone in particular?" she asked.

"Might," he said.

"You want me to heat you some breakfast up?"

"Yeah, thanks," he said.

After he polished off a plate of scrambled eggs and fried potatoes along with four pieces of toast, he washed it down with a half quart of orange juice. He ate a big breakfast as he probably wouldn't eat again until late that evening. He went into the living room and changed the channel from the videos that the kids watched to the news. All the kids hollered at the same time, "We watching videos, Jamal."

"I'm going to turn it right back; I'm just going to check something for a minute."

"Y'all not going to hog that T.V. with videos all day, I'm telling you right now!" Yolanda hollered from the kitchen.

"We ain't hoggin'," Poochi said sarcastically.

After about five minutes of watching the news he heard a horn blow outside. He looked out the window and saw the sky blue Honda; it was Byrd, who for good reason didn't want to get out of the car.

"Who is that?" Yolanda yelled from the kitchen.

"It's for me. I'll be back in a few to go shopping," Jamal hollered back on his way out the door.

He hurried out of the house, hoping they could pull off before anyone spotted Byrd. As they sped off, Yolanda, curious, looked out the window and saw that it was Byrd; she shook her head and mumbled. "Some people never learn."

"Did you get that for me?" Jamal asked Byrd.

"That's where we're on our way to now, to pick up Blood, he's going to hook you up. Knowing you just got out, he thought I was trying to play him for the gun, so he told me to bring you along; he didn't even know you had got out."

"Me and Blood was up north together before you came up there."

"Yeah, that's been awhile, huh?"

Byrd pulled up in the driveway of an old rundown house and blew the horn. A big heavy-set, dark-completed man stepped out of the house. He looked ferocious, beastly looking with battle scars all over his face; he hardly even smiled, a killer for sure. He trusted no one. He came to the car, immediately climbed in the back seat, and said, "Let's do this."

He gave Byrd directions, then spoke to Jamal, "I see they finally let you up outta there."

"Yeah, they had to. I maxed-out."

"It's good you're out, man; we need some real solders out here."

"Yeah, I can see," Jamal said.

They rode the next couple of miles in silence. Byrd turned in to an alley, stopped, and parked the car. Blood got out and told them to hang loose, he'd be right back. He cut through a path and disappeared. When he returned he had a duffle bag in his hand. Jamal had the door already open so he could climb right in with as little trouble as possible. Blood told Byrd to hit the freeway so as to lessen their chances of getting stopped by the police, as he was keenly aware of the present situation: three ex-felons with a car full of loaded guns; Byrd wanted for questioning in connection with the motel murders; Jamal fresh out of prison with a conviction of a cop shooting and he himself with outstanding warrants, one for a gun charge and one for a murder charge where he had been fingered as the trigger man. It could turn into an ugly situation if stopped by the law.

Blood passed the duffle bag up front and told Jamal to take the .45 out and pass the bag back to him. As Jamal opened the bag he saw three other guns besides his .45. He figured Blood was either selling them or he himself was going on a mission.

"Here you go, Blood, good looking out," Jamal said as he passed the bag back to him.

"Ain't nothing, dog; glad to be of some assistance." He had a high respect for Jamal and any man that went up state and took his weight like a man and carried his own.

Byrd took the ramp that would exit him off the Jefferies freeway and wind up at Jamal's house in a matter of minutes.

They reached Twenty-third street, Jamal lived right off the corner as they came off Buchanan, right in the heart of The Pit. They pulled up in front of the house. Jamal got out first and Blood handed him the duffle bag to put in the front seat, as he took no chances, then he climbed out from the back seat, gave Jamal the gangster hug, climbed in the front, and he and Byrd drove off with hopes they went unrecognized. However, Yolanda had gotten a glimpse of Blood when he stepped out of the car, and her heart raced a beat faster as she was now convinced that Jamal was back into the business or soon planning to be. Jamal had cut a hole in the inside of his jacket so he could conceal the .45.

Yolanda could not contain herself any longer; she felt compelled to confront Jamal about the company he was keeping. She waited for him to come out of the bedroom.

"Jamal, you know I hate to meddle into your affairs, but you're messing around with the wrong bunch for someone just coming home from prison. Byrd is bad enough, but the other monster, Blood Lawson, he just gives me the creeps." Then she added, "You keep fooling around with these maniacs and you're going to wind up right back where you came from, I'm telling you."

She had a point to a certain degree, he reasoned to himself, as at any given moment in that car he had just gotten out of, the situation could have turned ugly had the cops stopped then, and he would have been dead in the middle of it, but he would defend his position to the fullest.

"I feel what you're saying," he told his sister, "but you got to understand that these dudes are the only ones I can really count on. They have access to things I need to survive in these streets. Just like if I get into a beef with some of these young dudes that hang in crews, those same people that you're talking about are the ones that'll come to my rescue. This is something these white folks don't understand because they don't live in this environment. They make it a condition of parole not to associate with known felons; well when you've been locked up most of your life, you don't know anyone else but felons. And to make it a federal offense for an ex-felon to be in possession of a firearm and having to be in these streets unarmed is an act of suicide; these fools shoot first and ask questions later."

It was hard for Yolanda to refute what he was saying, being that she herself lived in that type of environment, even though she didn't hang in the streets.

"Well the least you could do is pick the lesser of the evils; you went to the bottom of the barrel," she stated and left for the kitchen.

He was thinking, it really was going to be rough. He was thirty years old and had no place of his own, didn't even have his own transportation, He never liked having to rely on others for his livelihood, not even his family, but his situation at the moment left him no choice. Something in the back of his mind kept telling him that it all rested on whether Cathy would be able to get him that job she was talking about. Hopefully if she did find one it would be time consuming so it would keep him out of the streets and lessen his chances of coming in contact with those who were involved in crime, then he could focus on the political and social aspect of changing conditions and plug into the global struggle against imperialism that plagued most of the Third World and affected his people right here on American soil.

A car pulled up into the driveway, and Jamal looked out the window; it was his nephew Raymond. He had gotten a lot bigger since the last time he'd seen him, which was about a year and a half ago when they had come up to visit him at the prison. When Raymond came through the door, his eyes lit up as he saw Jamal sitting in the chair. He had a great admiration for his uncle.

"Awe naw! What's up, dog?"

Jamal stood up and they greeted each other joyfully, "Long time no see."

"Yeah man I was just telling some of my dogs about you."

"I see you got a little size on you now. I guess you're ready for the world?"

"Yeah I'm ready for whatever," Raymond said.

"Hold up, I didn't mean it like that," Jamal checked him.

"Well ain't no use in me faking; I'm trying to get paid out here."

"So what you doing?"

"I'm slinging like everybody else."

"You're a follower then?"

"Naw, but that's the fastest way I know how to get paid."

"But who are you getting paid off of?" Jamal pushed on.

"Whoever buys from me."

"What if your little sister buys from you? It's still about getting paid, huh?"

"Well I wouldn't sell to her."

"But what if she's closet smoking and sends someone else to cop for her?"

"They say what you don't know won't hurt you."

"And what if you find out?" Jamal was digging deep to make his point.

"Well I, uh, you know, uh, would have to deal with that when I run across it," Raymond said, running out of defenses.

"The bottom line is you're going to be contributing to the destruction of your own people, as it may not be your sister but for sure it's going to be somebody's sister."

"I never looked at it that way."

"Man, can't you see what that shit is doing to our people? Turning some dudes that were real soldiers into zombies, turning respectable women into sluts, honest people into thieves, stealing from their own kind. The ones that are selling it are killing each other up over territories and through their greed and lust for obtaining more than the next man; they are tools of the system and don't know it, unconsciously carrying out the plan of genocide against their own race."

"How do you figure that?" Raymond asked.

"There is documented evidence linking the C.I.A. to the shipping of drugs into the U.S. through secret international cartels."

"Damn that sounds messed up. I wish I knew some other ways to make money like this," Raymond said, sounding halfway serious.

"There are; you just have to be in a position to do it. We'll kick that later; right now I need you to take me downtown so I can pick up a few outfits."

"No problem, you ready to roll?"

"Wait, let me tell your mama so she'll know she won't have to take me."

"All right, I'll be in the ride," Raymond said.

Jamal came to the car a few minutes later and said, "Let's roll, man."

They went to a couple of the well-known stores, and Jamal bought a couple of designer outfits, some Adidas sneakers from Foot Locker, and some other sports gear. Raymond paid for it over Jamal's objection.

When they were finished, Raymond took Jamal around for a little tour of the streets. All you could see on some streets were cars pulling up to a certain spot and people rushing the cars to peddle their product right out in the open; on other streets people would walk up to the side of a house and get served. There were plenty of different methods, but all served the same purpose.

"You see what I'm saying now? Everybody's slinging," Raymond said.

"Yeah I see it, but I bet you won't see it in the white neighborhoods."

Raymond thought for a minute. He had no defense for that and all he could say is, "Yeah you right."

As he pulled into a gas station to fill the tank back up for his mother, he knew Jamal had illustrated some good points, but the money was coming in too good at the moment to even think about giving the business up. However, for him it was more than the money; it had become a way of life, with all the glamour, drama, and excitement it entailed.

"I guess we'll head on back now, I don't want to hold the car up all day," Raymond said.

As soon as they got into the house, Raymond asked, "Did anybody call or come by for me?"

"Yeah, whoever it was said that they'll be back later on to pick you up," his mother told him.

"Jamal, are you all set on what you needed to get?" Yolanda asked him.

"Yeah I'm straight."

Just then a horn blew; a blue Blazer was parked in front of the house with music playing so loud you could hear it a mile away. There was no doubt it was someone for Raymond.

"That's for me. I'll check you later, Jamal, and we can kick some more of that," Raymond said to Jamal on his way out the door.

The phone was ringing on the desk in the living room. Jamal was the closest to it but didn't like answering it as he hadn't quite gotten the feel of things yet.

"Jamal, would you get that?" Yolanda requested of him.

"Yeah I'll get it. Hello!"

"Hello, may I speak with Jamal?"

"Speaking, who is this?"

"Cathy."

"Oh how you doing? I didn't recognize your voice."

"That's because you had no faith in me contacting you."

"True, I've grown to believe nothing until it happens."

"Well this is real and it's happening at the moment. I contacted my father and convinced him that he would be doing a great service to humanity if he could help find a job for a highly intelligent fellow just being released from prison who I met on the bus coming home from school, and he told me to bring you by his office Monday so he could meet you."

"He wants you to bring me by?"

"Yes, dummy."

"Are you sure he, uh, won't—"

"Look, he's not like what you think."

"What time am I supposed to meet with him?"

"Ten o'clock."

"Let's see, we can meet at the library then at 9:00; it's on Woodward Avenue, not far from entering the downtown area. Anyone can direct you there."

"That'll be fine. I'll be there."

"See you then."

"Okay, bye now."

"That was for you?" Yolanda asked.

"Yeah, a possible job prospect."

"Oh that's good, Jamal."

"I am supposed to go for an interview Monday at ten o'clock."

I would take you, but I have to go to work."

"Oh I'm straight, I can take a cab."

"You need some money for cab fare?" Yolanda asked.

"Naw, I'm all right. I had a little money saved up," Jamal said, going to his room.

He took off his shoes and just kicked back on the bed thinking: Problem number one solved; ·he had gotten the gun. Problem number two, he had no real money to support himself, he had no transportation, and could not afford a place of his own. What if the job prospect that Cathy so earnestly tried to arrange for him didn't come through, as her father might not particularly care for him? What would he do! A lot of men getting out of prison went straight to the welfare office, but his pride would not allow him to accept anything he could not pay back. He refused to sell drugs as he would not contribute to the destruction of his race, He did not want Byrd to line anything up, as it was against his principles to rob his own people. His only other option was to extract money from the rich whom had obtained their wealth by exploiting the labor of the workers and by cheating the common investors out of all their money; he had no problem in taking from those who by deception had robbed the common folk out of their earnings. So he had taken the attitude come what may, as he now understands why so many ex-felons returned to prison: the choices were thin. It was a trap; in the first place what prison actually prepared you for was a safe return back to the complex, but he still would try to dodge the trap. It all boiled down to whether he could be trusted for the job, so all he could do was look for the worst and hope for the best. He would spend most of Sunday just chilling around the house as he didn't want to go out into the street and jeopardize his chances of possibly getting that job.

He pulled out some books and material with that for the rest of the night undisturbed.

Sunday morning was a busy morning around Jamal's house, as Yolanda and the kids were getting ready for church. Yolanda cooked a big breakfast and would cook a big supper; their lunch would be eaten at the church, The whole family with the exception of Raymond and Jamal, would attend church services with Yolanda's mother out in the suburbs and then visit during the evening.

"Jamal, you going to church with us?" Poochi said.

"Naw, I ain't going to no stupid church."

"Why I got to go?"

"Because you grandmamma wants you to go with her."

"Raymond ain't gotta go," Poochi said with contempt.

"When you get to be his age you ain't going have to go either."

"All right everybody, breakfast is ready," Yolanda hollered from the kitchen. "And wash your hands before you come in here," she added.

Once everyone was seated, they all bowed their heads, with the exception of Jamal, while Yolanda said grace. Jamal hated this part of the meal, which is why with the exception of Sunday he preferred eating alone. A disgraceful act, he thought to himself, everybody sitting around with their heads bowed like a bunch of slaves praying to a spook. Damn its been four hundred years; hadn't they come up out of that yet? Well in due time he would break them from that, he calculated.

After they finished, everyone helped with the dishes as the one thing Yolanda stressed was keeping a clean house, even in the midst of a poverty-stricken neighborhood.

"Is everybody ready to go?" Yolanda hollered, coming out of her room looking like a fashion model. She was dressed in a powder blue tight-fitting top, almost putting you in the mind of a halter top, also fitted in a black leather skirt, a little tight and short for church, and a pair of black Versace high heels. On her wrist was an was an expensive gold-inked bracelet to match the gold-linked chain around her neck; she was indeed an eye-catcher.

As she and the kids were leaving she hollered back to Jamal, "Sure you don't want to join us? It might do you some good, you know."

"Naw I'm good right here, gives me time to meditate."

"All right we'll be back this evening," she said, shutting the door behind her.

He felt relieved now that he had the whole house to himself. Solitude was his favorite form of relaxation, something he acquired in prison by doing a lot of hole time. The first thing he would do was his exercise routine that consisted of jogging on the school playground which was only a block away, then do pull-ups and calisthenics, come home, take a shower, and meditate for about a good hour or so, then get into his studies. He pretty much kept the same routine he had in prison.

The school playground had a pretty big field, so he could definitely get his run on. As he jogged he noticed that people were out and about, but something was missing—that joy that people used to have was gone. You could feel it; everybody seemed to be strictly business in this neighborhood. Nobody was out just hanging around; everybody was either coming or going to handle some type of business. It definitely was not a friendly atmosphere. It kind of gave you a creepy feeling. If no one knew you, they didn't speak to you. Death seemed to be in the air. Damn, he thought, how things had changed in a decade. The only one's who seemed to have any life in them were the children. He couldn't wait to finish his workout and go back inside the house.

When he had finished his workout he stopped by the store on the corner and brought a forty ounce of Old English and went back to the house to shower and relax. After meditating for about an hour and a half he studied all the way up until the time Yolanda and the kids came home. They all ate supper together, and afterwards Jamal spent most of the evening listing to the news. He turned the T.V. over to the kids and retired to his room for the night.

Chapter 4

Monday mornings were hectic around the house, Jamal came to realize. The kids had to get ready for school, Yolanda had to fix breakfast and get ready for work, and he himself had an appointment for the morning; the baby also had to be taken to the day-care center. Yolanda had a heavy task, he thought; how did she do it? He admired her for her ability to support and run a household all of her own doing. All Raymond did was pay someone to do the landscape work, and he would come in periodically and do some work around the house.

Jamal decided to let everyone get out of the way before he took his bath, ate breakfast, or anything else since his appointment wasn't until ten o'clock and it was just six in the morning.

"Are you all set, Jamal?" Yolanda asked before she left.

"Oh yeah, I'm straight."

"Okay we're gone."

"All right," Jamal said as he went to take his bath.

He ate breakfast and listened to the news until a quarter to nine, and then he called a cab to take him to the library. He arrived at the library around 9:00 A.M. and waited for Cathy on the library steps while reading a book that he brought with him. He always kept some reading material with him so as not to idle away time. After about ten minutes he looked up and saw a white Cougar with a black vinyl top pull up in front of the library blowing the horn. It was Cathy. *Why does she have to blow that damn horn*? he thought to himself? It attracted too much attention. It seemed as though everyone on the street watched him go to the car; they probably were thinking he was her pimp. When he got to the car he hesitated a moment.

"Jamal, would you get in and stop looking around? There's no one watching us."

"Did you have to blow the horn? I could see you when you pulled up," he said.

"I was just making sure."

"You think we'll make it in time?"

"Sure, his office is out near Eight Mile Road."

"What kind of work does your father do?" Jamal asked.

"He's managing editor of a newspaper publication."

"Oh, I see where your interest in journalism comes from."

"Well, you could say there was a small influence along the way. What about your father?"

"My father! Hell he's been dead, got killed during the riots in sixty-seven."

"Who killed him?" she asked with interest.

"Who killed him!" Jamal repeated as if it was obvious. "The *police*," Jamal answered with a tone of bitterness.

"Wow, that's awful."

"Naw, what's really awful is that his hands were in the air when he was shot."

"They can't do that," Cathy blurted out.

"That's what I say, but they done it."

"Did your family file suit?"

"Yeah, they filed, but that don't correct the injustice."

"Well there wasn't too much more that could have been done."

"Oh there was more to be done, I was just too young to do it. I was a baby."

"That's why they have laws."

"The law only works in the interest of the rich and the powerful."

"Imagine if everybody took the law into their own hands."

"I imagined that when they shot my father."

They both fell silent for a moment. Cathy knew she had no way to win in a debate with him—he was much too sharp—so she broke the silence by getting off the subject. "We should be there in a few minutes."

"Yeah I want to hurry up and get this over with."

"Oh Jamal, it's not that bad. You're making it seem as though you're on your way to the electric chair."

"It would be quicker," he said and they both laughed.

"It was ten minutes to ten as they pulled up in the parking lot of the building Mr. Carrington's office was in.

As they stepped out of the car, Jamal noticed that there were mostly white people coming in and out of the building they were going into; there were a few blacks scattered here and there. They got on the elevator which took them to the fourteenth floor of the high-rise building where Mr. Carrington's office was located.

Once they reached the office, Cathy pushed the buzzer and the secretary buzzed them in to the office.

"Oh hi, Cathy, go right in. Mr. Carrington is expecting the both of you."

Mr. Carrington was sitting behind his desk with papers almost stacked to the ceiling when they stepped in. He was a tall man in his early fifties in fairly good shape for his age.

"Good morning, my dear. How's the world been treating you?" he asked in a joyful manner.

"I can't complain, Father."

"And this must be Jamal, the young man with the answers to some of the world's problems."

Damn, Jamal thought. *What the hell has she been telling her father about me?*

"Well sir, they say if you seek you shall find. I've sought and I've found, but I just can't seem to put them in the right places."

They all laughed.

"Now that's original," Mr. Carrington responded, immediately recognizing the quick wit of this young man. Cathy knew right away that Jamal had won her father over that fast.

"Well, getting down to basics, I have a job lined up for you at the Detroit Institute of Technology. Have you any experience at maintenance work?"

Wow! *What black man you know of don't?* he said to himself.

"Oh about half my life," Jamal said.

"Good enough then, they're going to need a man for the summer semester. I'll contact the school and let you know when they want you to start. I'm always in favor of helping out the less fortunate."

"Thank you, sir, it couldn't have come at a better time, as the seed of misfortune had just began to take shape."

"I understand you've just been released from prison?"

"Yes sir, quite a bitter experience."

"Well, I hope this will help set you on the right track, and if I can be of any future assistance, don't hesitate to contact me; here's my card."

He handed Jamal his business card.

"Thank you, sir, you've been a great help," Jamal said as he exited the office, leaving Cathy and her father alone in the office.

"Well, my dear, he appears to be a fine young man and very bright, but there's a certain coldness about him; it's in his eyes."

"Gee whiz, Dad, would you stop being so judgmental? The man's been locked up most of his life; he has a small bitter streak in him, that's all," Cathy said, defending Jamal.

"Well, you just be careful and don't put all your trust in him."

"Of course. Goodbye, Dad," she said and left the office.

Jamal was waiting in the lobby for her.

"You want to go have lunch when we get back?" she asked.

"Sounds good to me."

"My father was quite impressed with you," she said once they had gotten in the car.

"I was quite impressed with him. I really had expected someone totally different," he lied.

He knew Mr. Carrington was an undercover racist, but he was able to put up a good front in the presence of his daughter. He also knew that Mr. Carrington needed to fake a good deed in order to appease his conscience and rid himself of any guilt of contributing to the pain and suffering of people of African descent in this country caused by the system he represented.

"Where do you think we should have lunch?" she asked.

His mind was clicking fast; he was trying to think of a place where they wouldn't be too conspicuous. He directed her to a Coney Island downtown, the only place he could think of at the moment where they wouldn't look out of place being together. Downtown Detroit is where you can see people of all different ethnic groups mingling together, usually for business purposes, and then after working hours they would go back to their own separate lives.

As soon as they reached the downtown area, Cathy pulled up alongside a Coney Island Restaurant and parked the car. Then she and Jamal walked into the diner together with no one paying any particular attention to them. They found a booth near the back, more secluded to their liking. Cathy ordered hot dogs and chili fries; Jamal ordered plain fries.

"You don't have a big appetite, do you?"

"I ate a big breakfast, and besides, I don't eat meat,"

"A vegetarian, huh?" Cathy teased.

"To a degree; I eat fish," he said.

The place began to draw a crowd as it approached lunch hour in the middle of Detroit's business district.

"Well, so far Detroit doesn't seem to be that bad," she said.

"That's because you've just seen the downtown part. Detroit is a large city, and they got some rough spots that I'm even leery of going in, especially on the Eastside."

"Wow! That sounds exciting. I would like to see some of those places."

"I would like to show you some of them, but they really are dangerous; they are where the murders occur that are not reported."

"I have got a report to do over the summer for my journalism class, and if I could go undercover and be around some of these places, I could witness enough firsthand to turn into a fascinating report—the kind of thing that wins the Pulitzer Prize," Cathy said with excitement.

"I would very much like to see you accomplish that, but not at the expense of something happening to you. Police have gone undercover in some of those same areas and were never heard from again," Jamal said, making his point clear.

"Well, could you at least take me on a sight seeing tour? It's the part of the world that I and others like myself need to see, the part that is kept hidden from us."

"Okay I'll think about it," he said.

"This may all connect, considering where you'll be working."

"Oh yeah, how is that?" he asked.

"Well, the job is at a school for the disadvantaged."

"The disadvantaged! Who the hell is the disadvantaged?" he asked her.

"Those who by circumstance were not able to finish school and consequently were unable to secure meaningful employment." *She probably adopted those liberal terms from her father,* Jamal thought to himself.

"And the circumstances, I assume, are those who dropped out of school for whatever reason or had been expelled and of course those like me who are incarcerated at an early age."

"That's a fair assessment, but what I'm getting at is you can kill two birds with one stone."

"How's that?" he asked curiously.

"On the one hand you would be the maintenance man responsible for the upkeep of the building and at the same time you could attend school yourself, which requires registration and passing the S.A.T. test."

"The S.A.T. test! What's that?"

"The standard achievement test, the required entry exam in the educational system," she replied.

"Isn't that school located on the Eastside?"

"Yes, far east I think."

"Damn," he said, more so to himself, then he though, *I really got to pack a heater to put up with those idiots on the Eastside.*

They finished their meal with small talk, and she talked him into taking her sightseeing around the Westside of the city before she took him home. He was reluctant at first, but he decided to take her through a few neighborhoods so she could at least get a vague idea of the type of lifestyle that was lived on the streets of the ghetto.

He knew that in order to get the feel of the streets she would have to do more than just sightsee, she would have to spend at least a month out among the people. Right now he would just show her parts of the Westside, and if she could swallow that, then perhaps it would prepare her for a view of the Eastside where there are no holds barred.

First he took her to a neighborhood where heroin was heavily sold before he went to prison. It was still the same, just the drug had changed from *heroin* to *crack*. The neighborhood was in the Dexter and Richmond area, heavily infested with drugs and crime.

As they approached Dexter they could see crews of young men standing on the corners with their forty ounces of beer, just hanging out on the boulevard. When they got to Richmond they could see cars jammed up in the middle of the street as the young men rushed up to them peddling their merchandise. Cathy looked on in amazement; this was a new experience for her, like a scene out of a movie.

"Wow! This is incredible. It's like they're conducting a legal business. Isn't there any law enforcement around?"

"Law enforcement! Come on, some of them are your biggest pushers," Jamal said.

"I don't understand. I thought there was supposed to be a war on drugs," she said puzzled.

"The war is not on drugs. The war is on the black man who has the drugs; the drugs are just an excuse."

After turning off Dexter, he directed her to a neighborhood where people were virtually chilled out, where if drugs were sold it was not visible.

She made it to Grand River and drove around the area of Northwestern High School. Things seemed to be relatively calm. People just went about their business. The one thing she did notice about the ghetto: There seemed to be more of a free spirit than where she lived. People walked around eating barbeque ribs, kids ran up and down the street half dressed, people sat out on their stoops drinking beer and relaxing; you would see a group of men drinking wine and talking loud and nobody paid them any attention. There were no restrictions. You would see young guys hanging out their car windows with loud rap music coming from their CD's, men shooting dice in the alley, people just out doing their thing, with no certain way of doing it. They were poor, true enough, but rich in spirit. They could entertain themselves within that realm of poverty without having to put on any airs; you basically could just be yourself.

She had seen all she needed to see for that day, so she drove Jamal home. He lived a couple of streets over from the Jeffer's Freeway, so it would be easy for her to find her way home after hitting the freeway. As they pulled up in front of the house, a few of the neighbors looked on nosily, making Jamal a little nervous. Cathy thanked him for an interesting afternoon and drove safely back to Sterling Hights.

When Jamal came into the house everyone said, "Jamal, Jamal with the pretty white girl."

He knew they would tease him, so he tried to look serious and said, "Come on y'all, she's hooking me up with a job."

The kids started snickering, but Yolanda saved him by asking seriously, "You get a job?"

"Yeah, all I'm waiting for is a phone call to tell me when I start."

"That's good, Jamal, what kind of work will you be doing?"

"I'm going to be the new maintenance man at a school on the Eastside for medical students."

"What's the name of that school?" Yolanda asked.

"Detroit Institute of Technology."

"Oh yes, I heard of that one."

"Wake me up for dinner. I'm going to lay down for awhile."

For some reason he felt exhausted. He went to his room, shut the door, laid back on the bed, and fell asleep.

Chapter 5

Yolanda woke Jamal up at 5:30 for dinner, after she had fed the kids. She was serving spaghetti and meatballs, but she remembered he didn't eat meat, so she made his spaghetti without meatballs along with spaghetti sauce, greens, and cornbread.

She was a marvelous cook as she virtually raised a family by herself. Jamal and she sat and ate dinner together as they chatted about things in the neighborhood—who got married, who got killed in the last few years, who was doing all right by ghetto standards, who was fortunate enough to move out of the neighborhood to a better section of town, who had gotten a new car, who had gotten busted, who had the longest run without getting busted, how much the neighborhood had changed since he'd been gone, and last on the docket, how the police had gotten off the hook for the many cases of police brutality and corruption that lurked within the department with heads being turned the other way.

It all sounded like the highlights from a ghetto soap opera. However, while this conversation was going on, something was lurking in the back of Yolanda's mind. Feeling she couldn't contain herself any longer, she decided to bring the subject up.

"I don't mean to pry into your business, but that school where you're getting a job at, are you aware of the type of people that attend that school?" she asked with caution.

"Yes, I know, the disadvantaged," he said.

He thought about how he answered that and hated himself for doing so, as he realized he had gotten that term—or a term similar to that ones—from Cathy's father.

"No, I'm sorry, not the disadvantaged, but the advantage takers," Yolanda said sarcastically.

"What do you mean by that?" he snapped back.

"Most of the people who attend that school go just for the loan. The school offers a four-thousand-dollar loan. Most either use the money for investing in drugs to peddle it or spend it on consuming a drug. In other words, what you're coming in contact with is a school full of dope pushers, crack heads, dope fiends, petty hustlers, and ex-cons—hardly an environment that you need to be around coming out of prison."

Jamal recognized his sister's concern for his well-being, but at the same time she had nothing to offer or recommend in the line of immediate employment. He was not the type to just lay around and live off the fruits of others. He was always one to make his own way, whether legal or illegal. He would not even accept welfare as most prisoners did when coming home from prison.

"I understand what you're saying, and you have a valid point, but I don't have the patience to be out there searching for no job, getting rejected on account of my record and recent incarceration," Jamal stated.

"Well I hope you've worked on your attitude some; I would hate to see you allowing yourself to get provoked into something violent." Yolanda was referring to some of Jamal's violent outbursts when he seemed to get pushed to a certain point. He could be cool and calm one minute, then all of a sudden go on one of those violent sprees, injuring four or five people with the possibility of someone even dying. But over the years of his incarceration, at least the latter part of it, he had been able to control that violent urge that seemed to pop up in his moments of frustration.

"Yeah, I been working on it, Sis," he said while trying to visualize the situation he would be placed in at his new job.

"Well good luck. I hope you make the best of it," she said, getting up from the table.

"Red!" she called. "Get in here and clear this table off and wash the dishes when Jamal is through eating."

"Aw Mama! They getting ready to play Eminem's new video."

"Girl, you better get your butt in there and do like I told you."

"Jamal, you through eating yet?" Red asked.

"Yeah Red, come on, you can start now."

Jamal got up and went into the living room. As soon as he sat down, Raymond was coming through the door. "What's up, Jamal?"

"Nothing much, what's going on with you?"

"Just trying to make it, you know."

"Yeah I see," Jamal said, eyeing the large platinum chain draped around Raymond's neck. Raymond noticed Jamal eyeing it.

"Aw that ain't nothing, man, just something to keep my front up."

The chain had to cost at least eight to ten thousand dollars, Jamal estimated. "How much did you pay for that?" he asked Raymond.

"I paid seven grand for it, but it cost like twelve."

"You paid seven grand for that, and you don't even have your own car?"

"I'm saving for that now."

"Damn, what kind of car you plan on getting?"

"A Lexus LS 430."

"Man, you're hustling backwards. You already spent enough money to have you a little hoopty and your own place and you still living with your mama and driving her car."

"I offered her some money, but she wouldn't take it."

"You know damn well she ain't taking no dirty money. If you had a job it would be different; she wouldn't know where it was coming from."

"She could've acted like it came from her own job."

"Your mama is pretty smart; she don't believe in taking chances of that sort. Every dollar she makes she can account for, so when the I.R.S. steps down on your ass, which they're going to do in due time, they won't be able to link her to anything."

"Damn, why you say they coming down on me?" Raymond asked curiously.

"Because you're giving them every reason to," Jamal answered.

"How you figure that?"

"First of all you're making all this money, spending it lavishly, with no visible means of support," Jamal explained. "Secondly you're advertising what you're doing."

"Advertising!"

"Yeah, I been gone thirteen years and know what you're doing without anybody having to tell me. So if I can tell what you're doing in that little time, it wouldn't take a rocket scientist to figure it out, be he crook or not."

"Wow man! I never looked at it like that," Raymond said.

"You better start paying attention to what's going on out here. These white folks are letting these young brothers make all this money in the drug game while at the same time plotting their destiny."

"What you mean?"

"Man, you don't see all these proposals being put forth? They're going to strip these young drug dealers of everything they possess and then hit 'em up with so much time their shoes are going to run off and leave 'em. Before I got out, a young brother from across the way came through; I knew his brother before he got slumped. Man, look, they gave that young brother so much time he's still in a daze; he don't know whether to shit or go blind—first offense, too," Jamal related with a bit of humor and sympathy. Yet the message was clear: the system was strict when it came to dealing with people of African descent.

Raymond digested this raw. He really never figured he himself would go in to prison, even though his uncle had gone. Unlike his uncle, he sold drugs; whereas Jamal had confronted the system head on by robbing one of its establishments. However, Raymond never visualized himself getting caught selling drugs; he figured himself to be too crafty—in his eyes only a dummy would get caught with some drugs or selling them (being totally unaware of the drug conspiracy laws). He was like most of the others who peddled the drug, only looking at the money aspect of it and never weighing the consequences. Even though Jamal had made him consciously aware of what he was up against, he still somehow believed he'd come out on top.

"Yeah I gotta meditate on that," Raymond said." "I'll get back with you later; you need anything?"

"Naw I'm straight right now," Jamal said.

"Well here's a few ends anyway, something to help you until you get back get on your feet," Raymond said while dropping a wad of bills in Jamal's lap as he was heading out the door.

Jamal picked the wad of bills up and riffled his thumb across the top. He estimated it to be about fifteen hundred. *Well*, he thought, *I certainly could use it.* He wasn't like his sister—he was a straight-up outlaw; most of his money came illegally anyway. Whenever he came across some money (which he knew he eventually would and so did Raymond and everyone else that knew him), he would set Raymond straight for looking out for him; that was the street code.

Jamal now was thinking over what Yolanda said about the school. Cathy probably had no knowledge of what type of people attended the school; all she knew was that most were poor and hadn't had a chance to realize their potential. However, her father was an associate of the man who owned the school—a billionaire who'd feigned benevolence to the African American's education, which was a hoax in order to draw the interest off the student loans which were at high interest rates.

Jamal didn't adhere to that aspect of the school's program, as he was diametrically opposed to any form of the capitalist idea. But right now he would have to ride it out if he planned on obtaining employment for the moment. However, he had other plans also; he just had to put his priorities in order.

He went to his room and attended to his daily studies. There was no need to set the alarm clock as he had nothing in particular to do the next day. He opened some books and began studying, which occupied him for the rest of the night.

The next morning everyone in the house was up and about except Jamal. He was awake, but preferred just to stay in his room until the house was empty and everyone had gone about their daily schedule.

There wasn't much to do, so he went and grabbed the plate of food Yolanda had left for him and brought it in the living room to eat while he watched the news. He watched the news until about nine o'clock and then began to clean up around the house when the phone rang.

"Hello! Who is this?" Jamal asked.

"This is Cathy; I'd like to speak to Jamal."

"Speaking."

"Oh I thought that was you . . . I wasn't sure."

"There's nobody here to answer but me; what's up?"

"I'm just calling to let you know that you are to report for work Monday of next week, 7:00 A.M. at the Detroit Institute of Technology, 751 Miller Road."

"It certainly is a blessing to have that out of the way, and I really want to thank you for making that possible."

"Think nothing of it. I feel relieved knowing that you at least have a start," she said.

"Well now it's my turn; I'm a man of my word. If you're not doing anything tomorrow I would like you to report to the library for your introduction into the study of self-knowledge."

"Oh Jamal, you didn't forget! I can't wait—what time tomorrow?"

"How about one o'clock in the afternoon?"

"Sounds fine to me."

"Okay, I'll meet you there, same spot."

"I'll be there, goodbye."

Things began to shape up; at least half his worries were over, he reasoned. After he finished cleaning up, he put on his sweat clothes to get ready for his workout. He believed in staying in shape.

He went to the school's playground to jog as he had on Sunday. There weren't many people out and about yet, as it was still early in the day. You might normally see a few people out working on their cars or walking to the store or children out playing, but again Jamal did not feel that joy in the air as he once did before he went to prison.

When he finished working out he started toward the store to get forty ounce when he was approached by two younger men who were maybe in their teens or early twenties.

"Yo, big doe, you got that money you owe me?" the taller one said.

"Money! What money?" Jamal said arrogantly.

"You know from that package."

"Man, I don't know what you're talking about. I don't even know you," Jamal said as he attempted to push by the one talking to him.

He stood directly in front of Jamal and hollered over to the shorter one.

"Yo, this chump must think I'm joking."

Right then Jamal reached to grab him by the throat as the shorter one pulled a gun.

"Don't even try it, big dog."

Jamal, now realizing he was in a no-win situation, stood back, put both hands up, and said, "You got that, dog."

The taller one smiled and said, "You better get your punk ass on in that store," and gave Jamal a little shove on the way. Jamal went into the store without incident, keeping a clear picture of both of them in his mind, for they had violated and disrespected him in a manner in which must be settled. He would settle this even if he had to go back to prison.

Damn this shit is crazy, he said to himself. *You can't even go to the store around here without having to bump into one of these fools.*

After he got home he took a shower to cool off some, then he sat back in a living room chair with his forty ounces of Old English and began to reflect on what just happened. One thing he knew for sure: Those punks had to be taught a lesson. He didn't want to kill them unless they presented a threat. He wondered if his nephew might know them, they were around his age, but he really didn't want to tell Raymond because he was not a thinker, just like the two idiots he had just run across. Anyway, he always liked to handle his own business his own way. He thought about Byrd and Blood Lawson; they were on his level when it came to war strategy. Yeah, that was it—there was no more to even think about.

He beeped Byrd. He waited a few minutes and the phone rang. He picked up the receiver and on the other end, a strong voice came through.

"Yo who is this?"

"Jamal."

"Oh what's up?" Byrd said.

"I might need a little assistance.

"Is it urgent?" Byrd asked.

"Naw, naw, at your convenience."

"Well you know I don't usually come out until it gets dark."

"That's cool, just come scoop me when it gets dark."

"All right, no problem," Byrd said and hung up.

Jamal thought about the gun, "Damn." He had bought the gun for this very type of situation yet didn't even pack it with him when he went out to jog. Well maybe it was for the best that he didn't have it at that particular time as he might have been sitting up in the county jail right now with a murder beef. At least now he could plan things out.

He went into his room and pulled the gun from under his mattress and went outside in the back yard. He put the clip in and fired a couple of rounds. One thing was for sure and two for certain: He would not be caught without his gun again. He put the T.V. on and watched a movie to take his mind off things for a minute. When Yolanda and the kids came home he gave up the T.V. to the kids and went to his room and laid down until Yolanda had fixed his supper.

After he had finished eating he went in his room to pack his gun; he was going out walking until it got dark. First he went to the store hoping he would spot the two little punks. They probably wouldn't even recognize him again if they saw him; he was thinking that would give him the advantage. When he came out of the store he went around the corner and saw the little crowd that was peddling their product from a vacant lot across the street, and as fate would have it he spotted the taller one who had approached him about the money he owed him. He thought about taking him out right there, as the impulse hit him, but he would stick to his plan that he had arranged in his head; besides, there were too many witnesses.

He went back to the house; his mission was accomplished, at least that part of it. As soon as he stepped in the house Red jumped on him. "Jamal, where you went? To the store?"

"Yeah Red."

"Dang, I wanted to go."

"I didn't see you, Red; here take this and tell Wanda to take you." He gave her a dollar.

"Thanks Jamal," Red said as she ran to get her older sister.

It would be getting dark in about an hour, so Jamal went and packed a few things, as he planned to rent a room at the Cadillac Motel for a few days, maybe longer if the situation called for it. After he finished packing he told his sister that he would be gone for a few days and if anybody called, to take a message. He sat in the living room watching T.V. when he finally heard a horn blow; he knew it was Byrd.

"Bye Jamal," the kids said as if he was going away for a long time.

Yolanda came to the window as they were driving off. She couldn't make out who it was as Byrd had switched cars.

"So what's up man?" Byrd asked.

"First take me to the Cadillac Motel so I can rent a room; it'll be more comfortable to talk there."

"Damn! It's popin' like that?" Byrd said.

"Yeah, ain't no question."

The Cadillac Motel wasn't far from the house on Twenty-third, but where it was located you could enter without hardly being seen, ideal for Byrd.

Byrd pulled into the motel's parking lot and drove towards the back so as to keep out of sight as much as possible. Jamal got out and walked the distance up to the office. He came back with a key to a room as close to the back end as possible. Byrd waited until Jamal had entered the room before he even got out of the car. He got out, pulled his collar up, and moved swiftly to the room unnoticed. Jamal left the door cracked for Byrd. As soon as Byrd entered the room he immediately checked the bathroom with pistol out, the closet and finally under the bed.

"Goddamn Byrd, ain't nobody in here."

"Could be bugged, you never know," Byrd said as if he was expecting something to happen at any moment.

"Yeah I feel ya," Jamal said, understanding Byrd's paranoia.

"Well this is what's up." He related the incident to Byrd.

"So what you want to do, smoke 'em?" Byrd asked.

"Naw, you know I ain't into killing our own people unless I ain't got no choice or if they're collaborating with the enemy."

"Man, you on that revolutionary stuff hard, huh?"

"Yeah that's what I live for."

"Anyway this is what we gone do." Jamal related the plan to Byrd.

Byrd had no problem with it. "Yeah, well I can fill Blood in on it and we can go handle that tomorrow night."

"That's a bet," Jamal said.

"Here," Byrd gave Jamal a twenty-dollar bill, "get a pint of Martel and some cups from that liquor store across the street. I'm going to chill for a minute and put you up on some chicks."

"Aight," Jamal said, taking the bill from Byrd's hand.

When Jamal came back from the store, he and Byrd had a few drinks and kicked it for a minute. Byrd got up and said, "Give me about fifteen minutes. I'll be back with them."

Jamal put the T.V. on the news. After about twenty minutes there was a knock on the door.

"Who is it?"

"Byrd."

Jamal opened the door and said, "Daaamn!" as he looked at the two females standing at the door with Byrd looking like they stepped right out of a player's magazine.

"Come on in," Jamal invited them.

It was obvious that Byrd was with the taller one as she still clung to his arm. Byrd introduced them both to Jamal, and he naturally ended up with Angie, the shorter of the two. They all sipped their drinks that Byrd had brought with him and joked and laughed for about a half an hour when Byrd announced. "Me and Kim's going to bounce. We'll be back in a couple of hours."

"Aight, I don't know about her, but I'll be here."

"Yeah right," Angie said, and they all laughed as Byrd and Kim were leaving.

Angie enjoyed talking with Jamal. He talked about things that weren't common in everyday conversation, and at the same time he was a very amusing. But there was no secret why she was there, so she just let it happen naturally.

Wow! she thought to herself; she hadn't enjoyed sex like that in years. But she knew she couldn't allow herself to become attached to any of her clients, for after all, she was a professional hooker who danced in a nightclub from which Byrd had plucked her at a considerable price. However, in spite of it all she really enjoyed herself with Jamal; he was so different. She really wished that they would have met under different circumstances. They took turns going to the bathroom to wash up and then sat on the bed and kicked it some more until Byrd showed back up to take her back to the club.

Jamal felt exhausted. He took a shower, caught some late news, and fell asleep with the T.V. still on.

Chapter 6

Unbelievable, Jamal thought as he rubbed his eyes. It was 9:00 A.M. unusually late for him waking up in the morning. Well what the heck, he didn't have anything planned until the afternoon anyway.

He took a nice hot shower to start his day off, then he went to a restaurant across the street from the motel and ordered pancakes for breakfast and a glass of milk. There weren't many people in the restaurant at this time of day as it was a little after 10:00. So he brought a newspaper and ordered some coffee to kill some time. It was 11:15 when he got back to the motel. He wished now that he hadn't set up to meet Cathy today as his mind was on what he was going to do that night. But it was too late now; he had given his word. He thought about last night. He had a good time with Angie; they were sort of compatible. Neither of them were attached to anyone; they were free to do what they wanted. The only thing that separated them was that she was doing it for money. He watched the news until 12:00 then he left to go to hail a cab to take him to the library.

By the time he reached the library it was almost 12:30. He was early so he sat on the steps and started reading a book he had brought with him. There weren't a lot of people that frequented the library, but there was always a lot of traffic and a lot of people passed by due to its location. Jamal would look up from his book every now and then and just observe the people as they passed. He would always try to sense the mood of the people; it was part of his studies. When the people became dissatisfied, they would be primed for massive resistance, he calculated from his studies.

The next time he looked up he spotted the white Cougar. Cathy was looking for a place to park.

I hope she doesn't blow that damn horn, he said to himself.

She finally found a parking space across the street. Man, she looked lovely as she stepped out of the car, Jamal admired. Heads turned as she crossed the street. He stood up as she approached the steps.

"Am I on time?" she said, coming up the steps.

"You're always on time," Jamal answered, looking her up and down.

They entered the library together and grabbed a table in the rear as they planned to be there awhile.

"Well here we are, professor. What is my first assignment?" she humorously asked.

"The first lesson in the field of obtaining self-knowledge will be on thinking for *one's self*, which of course means freeing the mind in the essence."

"Freeing the mind of what, may I ask?"

"Freeing the mind of some of the doctrines imposed upon you during your school years and of a lot of the propaganda that has been spread through the mass media. They have psychologically gotten most people in this country to accept capitalism, not only as the best economic system to live under but also the only one, never offering an alternative."

"And what would be an alternative?" Cathy asked.

"Socialism, Communism—"

"*Communism!*" Cathy blurted out with shock.

"You see what I mean? You've been taught like most others that Communism is an evil."

"Look at Cuba."

"What about Cuba?" Jamal asked as if now demanding an answer.

"Communism has caused it to dink into poverty," Cathy stated firmly.

"It wasn't Communism that sank it to poverty: it was the sanctions imposed upon it by the U.S. for Castro's refusal to bow down and kow tow to them," Jamal shot back with authority. "And even with that," he added, "there is no one starving or homeless in Cuba, something that can't be said for the U.S. with all its wealth."

Cathy was more eager now to study under his tutelage, realizing how much information he had concerning global affairs. She figured she could pump more information out of him by questioning his views rather than letting him initiate them.

"So what's so terribly wrong with the capitalist system?"

"First of all its very deceptive. It has deceived over half the world into believing that everyone has an equal opportunity to benefit from the gains it has produced."

"Well they do, don't they?" Cathy pushed for deeper explanation.

"Not hardly. Those gains came off the backs of the laborers whose labor was exploited by the capitalist who own and control the means of production."

"But we're talking about opportunity—everyone has the opportunity to become a capitalist," Cathy insisted.

"Another deception. This system operated through slave labor, which is forced labor, so the opportunity only applied to the slave master; never did it apply to the slave. It's impossible for the slave to own the plantation while still a slave. The inheritors of those slave masters are your capitalists today."

He left no room to counter; she would totally have submit to this subject. This man had an analytical mind, Cathy observed; he was hard to go against regarding certain subjects, such as history, politics, economics, and religion. He seemed to have everything down to the science.

"How, or should I say, in what way are these other systems any better?" she pressed on.

"Well if applied correctly and earnestly, it calls for an equal distribution of the wealth or an equal share into the profits, denounces slavery, and rids its labor force of any form of exploitation," Jamal answered with confidence.

"Okay, now where does this propaganda that you spoke of come into play?"

"For the most part through the media, who did a job on Karl Marx, the author of *The Communist Manifesto*, by making him into a villain, and those proponents who came after him consequently smeared the image of Communism throughout the world. As one philosopher and social historian, Sir Isaiah Berlin, put it, 'The world wouldn't be in such a snarl if Marx had been Groucho instead of Karl.'"

"Well if capitalism is so bad, why is it that this country is so successful in comparison to some of those countries living under the system you mentioned," Cathy said thinking she may have him this time.

"If you're speaking in terms of wealth it's because America has spread its wings beyond its shores to drain the natural resources from mostly Third World countries through the use of cheap labor which has helped to enrich its own wealth."

"How were they able to do that?" she asked curiously.

"Bribery. It's not hard to pick the leaders of some of those countries who would accept a handsome sum in exchange for letting America's multinationalists put their factories over there; however, in other areas America isn't doing so great. It has the biggest crime rate in the world; it is no longer a safe place to live; the kids are carrying guns to school instead of books as you can see from all the school shootings; drugs fill the school yards now instead of bubblegum and candy; workers are becoming frustrated in their jobs and are taking out their employers; people are rising up killing their entire families then committing suicide. Now everybody is wondering what has gone wrong. Well nothing has *gone* wrong; it was wrong from the gate, the inequality of the capitalist system has been realized. The violence that was inflicted upon the indigenous people of this land and the peoples of African descent from slavery up until the present day by the controllers of this nation and their many sympathizers in their quest for wealth and power is now coming back to haunt them," Jamal summed up.

After she had absorbed enough from questioning his views, she was ready to ask him the big question. "A very interesting thesis, now how do I come about this type of knowledge?"

"Logic and reasoning. Everything you hear, read, study, and absorb in terms of information, you must first look for the logic in it, meaning you must question everything; take nothing at face value. There are two doctrines that basically oppose each other yet are philosophically accepted as the governing laws of the universe: One is materialism, which teaches that everything, including thought, feeling, will, and mind, is explainable in terms of matter; the others is metaphysics, which is more speculative knowledge, often based on facts, yet they can't necessarily be proven, and usually found in spiritual or intellectual pursuits. So in order to gain some insight into the mysteries that have been kept from the common people, you must log on to these two worlds of study. I will refer you to some books and literature concerning those subjects."

"Thank you, I really will appreciate that," Cathy said as they got up from the table and went over to the bookshelf.

After Cathy had selected some books, they went back to the table for some quiet study until about three-thirty. Cathy looked at her watch. "Oh wow, how time flies. You want to go grab something to eat?" she asked.

"Yeah we can do that; matter of fact, since we're already close to downtown we can go to Greektown," Jamal said quickly before she made any suggestions.

"Oh yes, where they have a lot of little restaurants."

Jamal directed Cathy to Greektown, an area about a block long in the heart of downtown Detroit that consisted of a few Greek restaurants, dress shops, and stores. It catered to middle-and-upper income people; both black and white, who pride themselves in being able to pay more for their meals than the average working-class person, knowing that the food doesn't taste as half as good as in those ghetto restaurants at a cheaper price. Jamal really hated eating in Greektown, but it was one of the few places in Detroit where interracial couples were not frowned upon, at least not outwardly. They decided Tony's as the place they would dine at, as it was more secluded. They ate dinner, engaged in a little small talk, and Jamal was dropped off at the motel while Cathy made it safely back to the suburbs.

It was a little after five, so Jamal took a shower so as to feel refreshed. When he was through, he kicked back on the bed and began to go over his plan in his head. He hoped Byrd would remember to bring the masks, the duct tape, the magic marker, and the cucumbers. He did not want to beep Byrd unnecessarily so as to add any suspicion to Byrd's already high paranoia.

After he felt he had the plan down pat, he turned on the news and relaxed. After nearly an hour of watching the news, he heard the knock on the door.

"Who is it?" Jamal asked.

"Byrd and Blood."

As he opened the door he saw the eagerness in both their eyes. They were both drama prone. Their lives were filled with high-drama situations. The risk in what they did was their high. Blood neither drank, smoked, nor got high; this was his high. He had been in more shootouts than Billy the Kid. Byrd drank and that was it, probably due to his nerves, as there always seemed to be someone after him.

"Did you bring everything, Byrd?" Jamal asked.

"Yeah, it's in the van."

"All right, we ready to roll."

They went over a few small details and left for their mission. When they reached the van, Jamal checked the duffle bag for the items he had requested; they were all there. Byrd drove the van the long way, where the streets were lit up, to avoid unnecessary trouble. When he reached the store where Jamal had the incident, he parked the van on the side where the vacant lot was across the street, but down a little ways so when they made their move it wouldn't be so much in view. They sat and watched the lot when Jamal finally spotted his vic.

"That's him, Byrd, the tall one with the green jacket on and his little partner with the blue baseball cap turned backwards."

"Got 'em," Byrd said, getting out of the van. Byrd was not from this side of town, so he was the least likely to be recognized. When he saw the tall fellow he hollered, "Yo dog, what you working with?"

"I got twenties," he said.

"Man, I'm trying to get some halves or eightballs."

"Yo, we got that. Yo June, you still got that ball?" he hollered to his partner.

"Yeah I got whatever."

"Let's go to my van, I'm trying to spend," Byrd said.

All three walked to the van. As soon as they got to the door Blood stepped around from the other side, and Jamal kicked the door open.

"Get y'all punk ass up in there!" Blood said, grabbing each one by the neck.

"Aw man, why y'all doin' this?" the two said frightened. Jamal and Blood both had masks on. Jamal grabbed the tall one by the collar and pulled him up in the van; Blood almost threw Shorty up in there.

As soon as Blood got in, Byrd took off. Byrd had taken the seats out of the back of the van so the two youngsters would be made to lay face down. Jamal and Blood taped their mouths and their hands behind their backs. When they reached the alley where Blood did his disappearing act, he had Byrd drive down a little ways and pull up in a driveway at an abandoned house that had been burned halfway down. There they stripped the two youngsters buck naked, wrapped them up good with duct tape, then left them in the van and the three of them walked over to Blood's hideout and chilled until four o'clock in the morning.

They went back to the van, made up two signs, and taped them on their backs, took the cucumbers and stuck one each in their buttocks, took them to the school's playground, and left them in the middle of the field with the signs on their backs which said **WANNA BE GANGSTERS.**

Jamal wanted them dumped there in hopes that the school kids would find them to further their embarrassment. They were left with their shoes on, with the money they had on them left in their shoes so as to indicate that this was no robbery. The drugs they had on them were crushed in front of them to let them know that this was no crack head move. Jamal never revealed himself as the guy they ran into at the store, as he lived in that neighborhood and didn't like leaving himself open for retaliation like they did. Blood wore the mask just for the hell of it. It didn't make any real difference to him if they saw him or not; he had so many beefs he didn't come out anyway, and most who knew of him would rather not go up against him, for not only was he gruesome, he was cunning in street tactics when it came to warring in the streets.

Byrd drove the van back to Blood's hideout spot and switched to his car and drove Jamal back to the motel to drop him off, then he headed off to the Eastside. Jamal took a quick shower and went straight to sleep.

It was Thursday morning around ten o'clock when Jamal woke up. The first thing he thought about was whether anyone discovered the two young men who were left on the school's playground. He decided to turn the T.V. on to the local news and watched it for about fifteen minutes, but nothing in regard to that came across the screen. He would have to go back into the hood to find that out, but it was risky right now as he could not say for sure whether the two victims could make the connection that what happened last night was a result of what took place at the store that Tuesday and could possibly recognize him if they saw him again. He could not afford to take that chance. He would wait until it got dark and slip back to the house on foot. He was not afraid of the dark; he had done some night-creeping himself back in his younger days.

He showered and went across the street to have a cup of coffee and get a newspaper. There was nothing in the news regarding last night's episode. *Well,* he thought, *if the victims were not found until sometime this morning it wouldn't be in the newspaper until the next day anyway.* After he finished his coffee, he went outside and hailed a cab. He was going to spend the afternoon downtown, eat lunch, take in a movie, get a haircut, and just basically kill some time until it started getting dark.

He caught the bus back to the hood. There was a bus that ran straight down Buchanan. He was really getting the feel of the city back. When he reached the hood he got off the bus two blocks before he got to Twenty-third, walked up a block to the next side street, and then walked back down to his house. That way nobody could pinpoint him.

When he reached the house the car was gone, but there were lights on in the house; he figured Raymond probably had the car. The kids were watching television when they heard the knock on the door.

"Who is it?" Wanda asked.

"It's me, Jamal."

"Oh!" she said as she opened the door.

"You walked over here?"

"Yeah from the bus stop."

"What bus was you on?" Wanda asked.

"The Buchanan bus; I caught it from downtown."

"Who is that?" Yolanda hollered from the kitchen where her and her friend Kisha were talking.

"It's Jamal," Wanda hollered back.

"You could let somebody know you were back, Jamal," Yolanda hollered out.

He could hear some laughter coming from the kitchen.

"Who's in there with your mama?" Jamal asked Wanda.

"Kisha."

As he was going to his room he hollered in the kitchen, "Y'all wouldn'tna heard me anyway, the way y'all rockin' it in there."

"If you would have heard about those two fools they found on the playground buck naked with nothing but their shoes on and a cucumber up their butt wanting to be gangsters, you'd be rockin' it too," Kisha said, still laughing.

"Yeah, when that happen?" Jamal asked, now standing in the kitchen doorway.

"They found them this morning; you'll see it on the news," Yolanda said.

Jamal went to his room to reflect on what had just happened. Did people really get the message, or did they think this was just some drug-related deal gone bad? He searched his mind for the answer. It had been quite amusing to Yolanda and Kisha; of course, they may not have grasped the full significance of the ordeal. He yearned to tell someone of what the whole thing was over, but that wouldn't look good for the image he wanted to project coming from prison.

A car pulled up in the driveway; Jamal could hear it from his room. Then he heard someone come bursting through the door, and he knew right away that it was Raymond, as that was the way he always entered the house. Like most of those around his age, they sought to make their presence known.

"Did y'all hear about Lil Cav and Muke?" Raymond asked his mother and her friend as he gave his mother the keys.

"Yeah we heard about them, and you're going to hear about something else," his mother told him.

"What?"

"I thought I told you to have the car back before it got dark; you know I got to take Kisha home."

"I know, Mama, I got tied up. I had to go pick up Tyneeta's baby all the way from the Eastside."

"Well you better get it together. I'm not going to let you hold me up. I got too many things to do; let's go, Kisha."

After Yolanda and Kisha left, Jamal came out of his room and went into the kitchen to find out what Raymond had heard about the incident.

"Hey, what's up, Jamal?"

"I didn't even know you were here."

"I just came in right before you did."

"Yeah, so what you been up to?"

"Nothing much, just gettin' the feel of the streets."

"Yeah, it's whack out here, man; you heard what happened up on Buchanan?" Raymond questioned to see if Jamal had heard.

"Yeah something about they found two dudes on the playground tied up buck naked with a cucumber stuck up their butts."

"Oh you heard!" Raymond said with excitement.

"I didn't hear what it was about; I just heard how they was found." Jamal fished for more information.

"Don't nobody know for sure, but everybody figured they must have really violated somebody."

"Don't nobody know who did it?"

"Naw, they say they were wearing masks."

Jamal felt relieved that he wouldn't have to take this any further When Yolanda came back, Jamal had Raymond take him back to the motel. As soon as he got to his room he put the T.V. on to catch the local news. He must have just missed it. He would have to wait until eleven o'clock. He flipped the channel until he came across a boxing match. He loved watching the fights as he had been in the ring a few times before he went to prison and even boxed a little while in prison until they banned it. He flipped back to the news channel after the fights went off. After about five minutes into the news what he had been waiting on came across the screen.

"*Two young men in their late teens were found naked with their hands tied behind their backs with an object stuck in their rectum on the McKinley School playground early this morning. Police believe that they were either sexually molest-ed or this was an act of revenge as robbery was ruled out as a motive due to the fact that large sums of money were still on their persons stuffed in their shoes, the only clothing left on their bodies. . . ."*

That was all he needed to hear; he could move on to other things now. He lay back on the bed to think about the job at the school. It wasn't the type of job that paid real money, but it was just something to feed and clothe himself and maybe get a hoopty to get around in. He thought it would be wise to go and check the school out before he started working there so he would have an idea of what the school was about. So he decided to drop by there sometime tomorrow since he didn't have anything to do. He did a little reading and retired for the night.

Chapter 7

He woke up around six o'clock that morning, but since he had no need to get up, he rested until about nine. He showered and went to the restaurant across the street. He had acquired quite an appetite and ordered a big breakfast of toast and eggs, hash browns, grits, and a large glass of orange juice. When he finished eating he decided to take the bus downtown and then transfer to another bus that would take him to the Eastside where the school was located. At least this would familiarize him with the route as he anticipated catching the bus.

By the time he reached downtown it was 11:40. He caught the seven-mile bus that took him to French Road and transferred to another bus that took him to the school. He saw a bunch of people coming off their lunch break entering the school, so he just followed the crowd.

Yolanda was right: nothing but a bunch of thugs, dope peddlers, crackheads, and petty hustlers attended the school. It reminded him of the prison school. The students were wild, running all over the place, loud and vociferous, mostly black; the entire staff was black. He immediately came to the conclusion that this school was a front. One thing he knew for sure—he would definitely pack his pistol.

He wound up in the student lounge where some of the students ate their lunch, but actually it was being used as a hangout spot for those who just attended the school for the loan, hardly ever attending class, just long enough to sign in.

The teachers couldn't have cared less if the students attended or not, for they were there just for the paycheck. It wasn't hard to tell by listening to the conversations that nobody took the school seriously, Jamal concluded. He finally ran into the maintenance man he would be replacing; just a few years older than Jamal, he seemed to like the job, but he had found a better paying one in the suburbs. He filled

Jamal in on what the job generally consisted of and how the school was basically run. Jamal was unimpressed, but nevertheless he would accept it for the time being.

After touring most of the school he decided to go downtown to see what he could get into. When he reached the downtown area he thought about the N.A.A.C.P. convention being held at the Cobo Arena. Though he was not an advocate of civil rights, nor had he ever viewed integration as a solution to the black man's problems, he would be more of an observer than anything else.

He couldn't believe his eyes; most of the people who attended were there showcasing, showing off their newly acquired attire, others trying to sell their products. Some people were selling tickets to a one thousand dollar-a-plate dinner engagement; it all boiled down to one big fashion show. When he could stomach no more he headed toward the door, pushing his way through the crowd. Angry at what he had just witnessed, he stormed out of the building.

He went to the Renaissance Hotel to take in a movie until it began to get dark, as he didn't want to wait until it got late to get back to the hood, for the later it got the more risk you ran of becoming some ones else's target of gunfire. He caught the Buchanan bus all the way to Tillman, the next street over from Twenty-third. He could something was going on over on Twenty-third, as he could see the red lights flashing. As he approached Twenty-third he could see the crowd gathering around but could not tell just what was going on. He began to hear shouts of, "Let the man up!"

As he got closer he could see a couple of houses down where five or six policemen were stomping and beating a man on a porch. He immediately rushed up to the house where the action was. Everyone was hollering, but nobody tried to stop them. Jamal made the first move; he went up onto the porch and grabbed one of the officers' arms.

"Man, let that man up," Jamal said, pulling one of the officers back.

"Get back, nigger, before you get it," another officer hollered.

Jamal punched him in the jaw, and before you could wink your eye a fight broke out. Others from the neighborhood rushed the policemen and they called for backup. It had turned into a small riot. People on the street began turning over a police car, windows were broken out of other ones, and they set another car on fire. The situation was out of control. All of a sudden about twenty police cars showed up out of nowhere, and policemen jumped out in their riot gear, swinging clubs. A helicopter showed up above dropping tear gas canisters, and the crowd began to disperse. Jamal and two others were arrested and handcuffed and charged with assaulting a police officer and inciting a riot. They were taken down to the precinct and thrown in a cell, unattended to.

Everybody in the neighborhood was talking about the incident. Raymond came home immediately when he heard it had happened on the street he lived on.

"Yo, I heard it was a riot on Twenty-third. Where did it happen?" he asked his sister Wanda.

"A couple of doors down on the Jackson porch. They was chasing some guy on a motorcycle and he ran up on the porch slipped and fell and a gun dropped out of his pocket. That's when the police that were chasing him ran up and started beating him up, and everybody started coming around telling them to let him up, but they kept on beating him; that's when Jamal came up and grabbed the policeman's arm—"

"Yeah, Jamal came out of nowhere, and when the police pushed him back and called him a nigger, Jamal punched him and a big fight broke out 'cause some other guys jumped up on the porch and got in. Then people just went crazy, turned over a police car, set fire to another one, and a bunch of police showed up in their riot gear and a helicopter dropped tear gas from the sky."

"Where's Jamal at?"

"He's in jail."

"Where's Mama?"

"She went over to Kisha's. I think she's going to try and get Jamal out," Wanda told him.

Raymond was proud in a sense that his uncle was the one who had stepped up, but he didn't want to see him go back to prison. About ten minutes later a car pulled up in the driveway; it was Yolanda and Kisha. As soon as they stepped in the house all the kids asked, "Mama, Jamal getting out?"

"We don't know yet; they won't let anybody visit him."

"Raymond in his room," Wanda told her mother.

"Raymond!" she called.

"Yeah Mama."

"Come out here a minute."

Raymond came out from his room, brushing his hair. "Yo, what's up?"

"We're all pitching in to see if we can get Jamal out on bond."

"How much is it?"

"We don't know yet; he won't have a bond hearing until tomorrow, so I'll need you to be here tomorrow early."

"Awrighit."

Cathy was watching the news when the report of the riot came across the screen. She saw a scene from the riot in parts—the street was crowded with people, and it showed when the people were scattering from the tear gas and the police car on fire. She also saw the end when the police arrested several individuals, but you could hardly make out their faces. They gave no names of the individuals who were arrested. She remembered the street as the one Jamal lived on and wondered if he could have been involved. Her curiosity got the best of her and she called the Rush residence; the phone rang and Red picked up the receiver.

"Hello! Who speaking?"

"Cathy, may I speak to Jamal?"

"Jamal in jail," Red said.

"He's in jail—what for?" Cathy asked.

"The riot."

"Is your mother there?"

"Just a minute. Mama! The white girl on the phone."

Cathy heard her over the phone and thought that it sounded racist the way Red said it. Yolanda rushed to the phone, thinking that Cathy may have heard from Jamal.

"Hello!"

"Hello, this is Cathy, a friend of Jamal's. I just learned that he was in police custody and wanted to know is there any way I can be of some assistance in obtaining his release."

"Right now we won't know anything until tomorrow. If you can give me a number where you can be contacted, I'll get in touch with you."

"That'll work," Cathy said as she gave Yolanda her phone number.

Jamal woke up to find a sweet roll and a cup of coffee in the food slot of his cell. He couldn't bring himself to eat or drink as he'd gotten a swollen lip, along with a few other bruises on his body which he had obtained during the scuffle with police. Nobody had come to talk to him, question him, or anything. It really didn't matter; he was used to this sort of treatment for being in prison for the long period that he was.

Yolanda came down to the precinct that morning and was told that Jamal and the others were being detained under the Riot Act and could be held without bond until a determination was made, which was indefinitely. When she got home she contacted Cathy to let her know Jamal's status. Cathy was furious; they couldn't just hold somebody indefinitely; there had to be a time frame. She knew constitutional law, but she was not familiar with the Riot Act; she would have to contact some high-powered attorneys in a hurry in order to get Jamal released by Monday so he could report to his new job. *Why did he have to react violently?* she thought; *he could have just protested like everyone else.* Now he had jeopardized everything that they were working toward, but Yolanda did mention to her that Jamal had a quick and violent temper when triggered, especially when it came to dealing with police, whom he held responsible for his father's death.

The department was under critical fire. Inspector Crawford was just finishing up the last case where an African-American male was killed by white police officers in that same neighborhood. The officers who were responsible for this incident would have to be suspended, and the prisoners would have to be let go if enough pressure was applied from those outside agitators, he reasoned. The press was making a big deal out of it; the publicity was killing the credibility of the department.

When some attorneys showed up on behalf of the men being held they were told that there had been no charges filed as of yet and the men were just being held for questioning. This gave the department an out; the last thing they needed was a big trial to blow this thing up. The attorneys were stressing the seventy-two-hour disposition since the state of emergency was lifted under which the Riot Act applied. Jamal and the others were released Monday afternoon without even being questioned. It was all politics, he figured. When he got home no one was there so he immediately called Cathy to see if he still was able to get the job.

"Hello! May I speak to Cathy?"

"Speaking, is that you, Jamal?"
"Yeah it's me."
"Are you calling from the precinct?"
"Naw, I'm at home."
"You're kidding—they let you go?"
"Yeah just like that; I never talked to nobody."
"Listen, I called the school and told them that you had to report today to your parole officer and would be there tomorrow. They know you've been to prison, so they said it was no problem."
"How did you know I would be out by tomorrow?"
"I was the one who had the attorneys go up there and press the issue for your release or for you to be charged; it was a calculated risk."
"Well there it is—I'm indebted to you again."
"Oh stop it. That was just the human thing to do."
"Yeah I know, but I still owe you one."
"Well you can pay me back by meeting me at the library."
"When, today?"
"Yes, after you have gotten yourself together."
"Okay. Let's say about three o'clock."
"That'll be fine. I'll see you then, bye now."

The first thing he did was take a good bath, as he hadn't had one in three days. After he had gotten through with his bath and finished dressing, it was about a quarter after two, so he tried to catch the news to see if they said anything about their release from custody that afternoon. There was nothing said as of yet; it would probably come on that night, he thought. His name hadn't been mentioned; they were just referred to as the men arrested for the riot and he was glad for that. Now he wondered if anyone had recognized him on T.V. the night that it happened. He hoped not as it might ruin his chances of getting that job.

It was getting near the time of his appointment with Cathy so he wrote a note letting Yolanda know that he had been released and would be back home that evening. He called a cab and waited.

He arrived at the library around ten minutes to three, and to his surprise Cathy was sitting in the car waiting for him. As soon as' she spotted him she jumped out of the car and ran up to him. He felt somewhat embarrassed as people looked on.

"Are you all right?" she said excitedly.
"Yeah, I'm fine," he said. "Let's go inside," he added.

She grabbed a hold of his wing and they went up the stairs together. They grabbed a table in the corner once they were inside.

"That was a crazy thing you did, Jamal; you almost blew everything."
"I couldn't help it. I just couldn't stand by and let them beat the man."
"You could have just hollered 'Let the man up' like everyone else."
"To commit a crime is bad, but to stand by and let a crime be committed is sometimes worse."
"Oh Jamal, there was no crime being committed."

"It was a crime to me—they may have killed the man the same way they beat a black man to death a few years back in the same neighborhood."

"Yes I remember, and the officers were arrested, taken to trial, found guilty, and sentenced to long terms in prison."

"Yeah, but that's after the fact. I believe in stopping it before it happens."

"I can understand that, but I don't think they would have gone to that extent in front of those people."

"I bet you can't tell Rodney King that."

She knew that it was fruitless to go on debating that with him. "Were you questioned or beaten at the station?" she asked.

"Nope, we were thrown in a cell and fed the next day and that was it; nobody said a word to us the whole time we were there."

"I don't think they could stand the publicity of a trial. That's probably why they didn't charge anyone with inciting a riot."

"How did you find out about it?" Jamal asked.

"I saw it on the news."

"You saw my face!"

"No, just the back of your heads."

"And you recognized me from the back?"

"No dummy. I never said I recognized you."

"Then how did you find out I was involved?"

"I recognized the neighborhood and had a premonition that you were involved and called your house; your sister related to me what had happened."

"You don't think anyone saw my face on T.V., do you?"

"Not really. The T.V. cameras just caught the back of you as you were being shoved into the squad car."

"That's good, I definitely don't need that hype."

"I just wanted to see if you were all right. I don't want to hold you up. I know you have some things to take care of."

"Nothing all that important, but we can get out of here and go grab something to eat before I get started if you want to."

"That sounds good to me. Where to, Attila?" Cathy said and they both laughed. They wound up going to a Burger King, and Cathy drove him home afterward.

As Cathy pulled up in front of Jamal's house, Red spotted them first and ran into the house hollering. . . .

"Hey, y'all, Jamal out there with the white girl."

"Shut up, Red! I told you about that," Yolanda hollered from the kitchen.

Everybody else ran to the living room to look out the window. Jamal spotted them looking out the window and hoped Cathy hadn't spotted them. He wished her a safe trip, stormed up the sidewalk to the porch, and pushed the door open.

"Damn! Y'all act like y'all ain't never seen a white girl before," he said, a little heated.

"We ain't looking at her," Poochi said sarcastically.

"Damn, sho ain't nothing else out there to look at."

"Jamal, would you come in the kitchen, please?" Yolanda hollered out.

"Yeah, what's up, sis?"

"Jamal, you need to slow down. You haven't been home a hot minute and you knocking on the prison door already."

Yeah, I know. I had a flashback when I saw them beating that brother."

"Well, man, you better fast-forward before you find yourself standing in the chow hall line again," Yolanda said dramatically, hoping it would take effect on him.

"I feel ya, sis. I'll bear that in mind if something like that comes up again," Jamal responded more or less to clear the air.

"What about the job at the school? Is it still available?"

"As far as I know, yeah."

"Well, maybe it'll turn out for the best, because I see right now you need something to keep you busy and out of them streets."

Jamal thought for a minute. He wondered if she knew about the other incident and didn't say nothing. Raymond could have found out and told her . . . well anyway, he wouldn't dare ask.

He went back into the living room, and all the kids wanted to hear from him about the riot incident. They all gathered around as he gave a blow-by-blow account of what happened out there that day. He told the story his way of how the police beat the man for nothing. Then he told them the story of how their granddaddy died in the riot back in the day and how black people were more serious then about the struggle. He talked right up until it was time for the kids to go to bed. This was his favorite topic; he was "ampted up," and the kids were soaking it up. Yolanda almost had to drag the kids to bed.

Jamal had no more audiences, so he too retired to his room for the night.

Chapter 8

Jamal awoke that morning at exactly five o'clock. He really didn't need an alarm clock even though he had set his the night before; it was normal for him to get up around that time. He went to the bathroom to brush his teeth and shower. The bathtub had a shower sprinkler above it so it was a matter of choice if one wanted to bathe or shower. Jamal always chose to shower in the morning, as it was a lot quicker. He knew the kids would be up soon to get ready for school, and he wanted to be out of their way; he could take a bath after he came home from work and then take as long as he wanted.

Yolanda was already up cooking breakfast and he thought to himself, *Damn, she must have been up since four or four-thirty.* Yolanda was very responsible person; she went to bed early, knowing she'd have to get up early and fix breakfast for everyone, get the kids ready for school, and then get ready for work herself. Jamal was dressed and ready for breakfast in twenty minutes. He was always fast and efficient at everything he did. When he stepped into the kitchen, the table was already set for him.

"You ready to eat?" Yolanda asked him.

"Yeah, you know I'm always ready for that in the morning."

She fixed his plate; she already knew what type of food he ate and didn't eat. He liked oatmeal, toast, and a cup of coffee to start his day off, especially if he had to go to work. He was always into trouble when he was coming up as a child, so work took the place of school for him most of the time. He had no problem with work; it just never seemed to pay enough for him, which is why he hustled on the side, which eventually led to bigger things that would land him in prison.

The phone rang; it was for him.

"Jamal, you're wanted on the phone." Yolanda hollered out.

"Hello!" Jamal hollered into the receiver, somewhat angry that someone would be calling him that early in the morning.

"Who is this?" he asked.

"Wow! Take it easy; it's only me, Cathy."

Relieved now to some degree he said, "Do you always call this early in the morning?"

"No, only when there's a primary interest involved," she answered softly.

"Could that interest be you checking up on me to see if I'm going to make it to the job?"

"Very good, you're catching on to me fast."

"Come on now, you didn't have to do that. If I tell you I'm going to be at a certain place at a certain time, you can take that to the bank."

"It's not that I lacked faith in your word, it's that in these types of situations anything possible could happen."

What type of situation was she talking about, he thought to himself. "Okay, I understand now, good looking out," he said to make her feel better about it.

"Really Jamal, I just wanted to see that everything went all right on your first day," she said.

"I appreciate that, but I've been up and ready to go. We can have lunch or something tomorrow, and I'll let you know how things went and if I like the job or not."

"That'll be fine with me. What time would you like to get together?" she asked

"I would say around six in the evening."

"Sounds good to me. Do you want to meet at the library again?" she asked.

"Yeah, that's the best place; it's like neutral ground," Jamal insisted.

He doesn't trust anybody, Cathy thought to herself. "Okay, take it easy and good luck, bye now."

"Goodbye," Jamal said as he hung up the phone.

"Hey y'all, Jamal up," Red said.

"We know, he got a job," Poochi said matter-of-factly.

"Mama, you taking Jamal to work?" Wanda asked.

"Girl, you know I can't take y'all over to Kisha's, drive all the way over to the Eastside, and still get to work on time."

Jamal overheard the conversation and told Yolanda, "All you got to do is drop me off on Michigan Avenue, and I can take the bus or catch a cab from there.

"All right, I'll be ready in ten minutes. All those that are not ready are going to walk that butt to school—y'all hear me!" Yolanda announced.

"Yeah Mama, dang, " someone hollered out.

At six-thirty they all piled into the car; she dropped Jamal off first at the bus stop, then she dropped the kids off at her friend Kisha's house who would take the kids along with her kids to school, and from there she would drive to work, killing two birds with one stone.

CHAPTER 9

Jamal arrived at the school around a quarter after seven. There were people already there, some staff he assumed. The school was relatively small for the number of people who attended. The only thing that made it look large was its long hallway that extended around two corners, but everything was all on one floor.

He was looking for a Mr. Johnson, the school's head administrator. The school's hall turned so many corners he forgot which way the office was. He decided to approach the young lady who was putting something up on the bulletin board.

Excuse me, Miss., could you tell me where Mr. Johnson's office is?" he asked, interrupting her.

"Why certainly," she said. "I'm his secretary, just follow me."

As he followed her he had to admit, she was well stacked.

"You wouldn't happen to be the new maintenance man for the school, would you?" she asked.

"Yeah that's me, at everyone's service," he said jokingly. She laughed and knew right away that she would like him.

"My name is Catrina, and you must be?"

"Jamal," he answered.

"Welcome to D.T.I."

"I'm honored to be here," he said rather gentlemanly.

"Well Mr. Johnson is not here, I see. Would you like for me to show you around so you can get an idea of what your job consists of?"

"Please do," he said.

She took him on a tour of the entire school, pointing out some of his job details along the way. By this time the students were coming in. *Man*, he thought to himself, *I see what Yolanda was talking about; these are some rough-looking characters.* They reminded him of the dudes he had just left in prison. He could tell the ones who were packing heaters—a street instinct. He could also distinguish by the way they dressed who was on drugs and who was dealing the drugs. He could tell the stick-up men and the killers by the look in their eyes. This was no doubt a school full of thugs and bangers. He would have to be very careful how he dealt with these dudes to avoid any altercations, especially over some female, as their presence seemed to excite the mass of male students.

Mr. Johnson finally arrived and was sitting in his office arranging some papers when Catrina entered.

"Good morning, Catrina, I see you got here early this morning."

He was very fond of Catrina, who was an excellent and loyal secretary to him. He really felt he could trust her. There were a lot of things that went on in that school that couldn't stand public exposure.

"Yes, I was fortunate to get the kids off to school on time this morning. By the way, the young man who was hired for the maintenance job is waiting outside of your office. I showed him his responsibilities; do you want to talk with him?"

"Yes, send him in. It'll just take a minute."

She looked outside and signaled for him to come in. "Mr. Johnson, this is Jamal, our new maintenance man."

"How are you, young man?"

"Fine, sir, how about yourself?"

"Well a little tired and overworked, but nevertheless, as they say in street language, *ready to roll.*"

Jamal had formed a quick opinion of Mr. Johnson already: a typical Uncle Tom with a house slave mentality, setting himself apart from the street people, living the illusion that he's accepted in the white world and far better off than the masses of his people.

"Catrina tells me that she familiarized you with the job pretty much?" Mr. Johnson stated to Jamal.

"Oh yeah, she was very efficient in doing that."

"Good then, that's settled. If there's anything specific that needs attending to in that line of work, you'll be notified through Catrina or myself. There's not a very lot to be expected from our employees here other than honesty—conduct of a higher standard in order to gain the respect of the students, who you will come to notice have a tendency to become somewhat rowdy at times from a lack of former discipline and who maintain a street mentality that doesn't conform to the usual scholastic environment."

"Oh, I understand," Jamal managed to get in.

"We will start you off at eight dollars an hour and a raise will be determined by your performance. All the necessary paperwork will be handled by Catrina. If you plan on attending the school yourself there is a Standard Achievement Test that is required. Once enrolled, you are eligible for a student loan up to four thousand dollars, payable upon your job placement after graduation or any job that you maintain or obtain. Are there any questions?"

"No sir, you've covered the waterfront," Jamal answered, glad that Mr. Johnson was finally finished.

"Okay then you can get started."

As Jamal left the office it wasn't hard for him to sense that this whole set-up was a scam with Mr. Johnson playing his role to the T, actually caring less about the students becoming educated or learning a skill toward meaningful employment, but rather to get the students to graduate and into one of the small clinics as a medical assistant, which doesn't pay as much as the job he's coming into, all for the sole reason of making the interest off the student loan. They even went as far as paying the students a hundred-dollar bonus to recruit people off the streets to attend the school.

The owner of the school, who was a white billionaire, played on the poverty and ignorance of the poor who in this instance, and usually most other instances, were black, Jamal concluded. Jamal attended to his duties while at the same time observing the school's activities.

A few of the students he observed were serious about their classes. They took up typing as the first step before going into computers in the field of medical word processing, which also included a course math, accounting, and English. The other field was medical assistant, which consisted of learning a lot of medical terminology and learning how to take blood samples. You could sleep through the course and still pass, Jamal figured.

He also noticed that the staff wasn't much more advanced than the students. It appeared to him that most of the teachers came straight from graduating from the same school and became teachers. He felt within himself that he was capable of teaching any of the classes they offered right on the spot; to attend the school as a student would be an insult upon his intelligence.

At lunchtime he went to the Burger King across the street from the school. He noticed that a lot of the students who attended the school ate their lunch there also. He ordered fish and fries and sat in one of the empty booths. When he looked up he saw a fellow coming his way whom he had known some place, *Ah*! he thought to himself, it was Champ, a fellow he had been in the joint with.

"Jamal! What's up, man?" Champ spoke in delight at seeing him.

"What's going on, Champ. I ain't seen you since the block. How long you been out?"

"Almost a year, when you get out?" he asked Jamal.

"Last week."

"I hope you ain't going to that ol' whack school across the street."

"Naw, I don't go to school there; I work there as the maintenance man."

"Oh yeah, that ain't bad; you just got to avoid running into a lot of them suckers. You ran into anybody that was up the way with us?"

"Yeah. Bird and Blood."

"Who? Blood Lawson?"

"Yeah," Jamal answered.

"Ah man, that dude Blood is on some Wild Wild West shit, he already had about four or five shootouts in the streets and ain't been out too much longer than me. And Bird is on some straight slumpin' jokers. They looking for him now about them motel murders."

"Yeah I know, but he's laying low, though; so is Blood."

"Them dudes is living on borrowed time."

"They'll be all right, though," Jamal insisted.

"Yeah, well anyway, what you really up to?"

"I ain't doin' nothing right now but holding this job down."

"Yeah me either, I'm just going to school to keep the press up off me; after I kick this parole I'll be ready for some action."

Champ knew Jamal's M.O. and was trying to bait him into committing himself to putting one off his licks down. Jamal was considered a professional stick-up man in the streets, but his most outstanding characteristic was that he was known to have a lot of heart and possessed a diehard mentality as one who sticks to the code. That reputation alone caused a lot of dudes in the game to want to get down with him. But Jamal had spotted the bait and quickly changed the subject.

"So what's up with this school? I mean you know how it's laying?"

"It ain't bad as far as getting your groove on with the chicks, but you got a lot of knuckleheads that go there, so you got to try and get around them to keep from catching a case. The staff is whack, a bunch of bleached-out house niggers trying to be important."

"Yeah I peeped that already," Jamal told him.

Champ and Jamal ate together and chatted awhile with a lot of small talk, then left and went back to the school together. Champ filled him in on everything he needed to know. Jamal felt more comfortable with dudes he had been locked down with than anyone else, even women, as the common bond of confinement overshadows most other relationships. He spent the rest of the afternoon doing what work was left to do and inspecting the materials the students used for their classes.

He inspected the typewriters that were used for typing class.

They were almost brand new, which would be ideal for him as he had done a lot of writing while he was in prison and never had the opportunity to type a lot of it up due to the large amount of time he spent in solitary confinement. He had written poetry, essays, short stories, and he was currently working on a book.

When he spotted the computers, he was quite elated in what he saw—it was a room full of new computers, hardware, software, micro, the whole works. He now contemplated taking up medical word processing that the school offered, which would give him unlimited access to the computers and typewriters. He also viewed this as the perfect opportunity to bring his political and revolutionary ideas into focus. He would work on getting a few of the students involved in some direct action against the oppressive forces that continued to hold his people down, The marching, rallying, and peaceful demonstrations he would leave to the moderates who didn't want to sacrifice much to gain their liberation. He understood from studying history, especially that of liberation struggles around the world, what it took to even be recognized as a liberation front. He knew you had to apply pressure that would be felt by the oppressive force before even being considered for any marginal gains toward liberation.

Since Detroit was leading the country in police brutality suits, he would use that as a focal point to base the immediate struggle around. He would begin to document every incident of that nature until he would find one to incite the back community at large. And if justice did not prevail, he would send his forces into action, as he pictured; no one responded to a bunch of rhetoric anymore, only action.

Once established as a protective force for people's rights, he would link his group to some of the legitimate, already accepted organizations. He would also establish a legal fund for the group, as he already anticipated charges being trumped up against them once they became effective.

This was no overnight dream of his. He had been prepared for this for years. His group was already established in prison. There weren't many, as he believed one good soldier was better than a thousand fake ones. So in his selection he chose the cream of the crop. And he would use the same method of selection now that he was out, even if it meant just one recruit.

His thoughts suddenly were interrupted by a need to use the restroom, and he happened to walk right into the middle of a drug transaction. The three men who were involved all looked up at the same time.

"Excuse me, brothers, just coming to take a leak," Jamal said as he passed by them.

They continued their business without a word being spoken. As Jamal left, one of the men spoke, "That's the new maintenance man that just got out of the joint."

"Yeah, they say he go hard," the other said.

"Ain't no doubt, you can look at him and tell that."

Jamal was six feet tall, one-hundred-eighty-five pounds, well cut for his size, dark skin with somewhat curly hair, handsome in a sense, but he had that hard-core prison look. He carried himself in a fearless manner; no matter how polite he was, his mannerism commanded respect at the door.

"We might have to watch it. He's a stick-up man, ain't he?" the one making the sale said.

"Yeah, but he don't stick dope boys up, he on revolutionary time," the other said.

It was nearly 3:00 P.M., classes ended at that time. Between 3:00 and 4:00 Jamal would tidy things up and the punch out at 4:00. When he got home he noticed it was about 4:45 P.M. So he figured tomorrow when he got off work he would go straight downtown to the library rather than come home first, as he never liked being late for an engagement. If Cathy showed up and he wasn't there she would probably leave anyway.

Yolanda would be home at any minute, she had to stop by Kisha's house to pick the kids up after she got off of work. To his surprise Raymond was in his room a sleep. *Very unusual,* Jamal thought, *he's hardly ever in the house much.* He spent most of his time hanging at the spot where they sold the drugs; the rest of the time he was just in the streets, the same as he'd done when he was younger. After thinking about it for a minute, he guessed that Raymond was probably waiting for his mother to get home so he could use the car after she'd gotten off of work, except on the days she went shopping. What was good for her was that she never had to spend money for gas, as Raymond made sure the tank was full when he brought the car home.

Jamal turned on the T.V. to catch the news before the kids got a chance to put on the videos. The first thing that came across the screen was about a massacre that had just occurred in the neighborhood he was living in, in a developing drug war. The first thing that came to mind was his nephew: *Was he involved in any way?* he thought to himself. He had not been hanging in the streets, so he really didn't know what was going on out there. If Raymond was involved it could jeopardize everyone in the household. He knew a lot of the fools who had gravitated to the dope game had lost any sense of morals and principles when it came to striking out at their adversaries in their senseless turf wars. Greed and a lack of respect for the right of the next person to do the same thing they were doing overshadowed any semblance of morality so much so that they would slaughter an entire family to send a message to their adversary. He went to Raymond's room and woke him up.

"Yo! What's up, Unc?" Raymond said as he turned over, his eyes beet red from what appeared to be a lack of sleep.

"We need to holler on some serious stuff," Jamal told him in a serious tone of voice.

"All right, let me freshen up a bit. I'll be right with you."

He went to the bathroom to brush his teeth and wash his face. When he returned they went back into his room in order to have some privacy in case Yolanda and the kids showed up.

"So what's up, Jamal?"

"First of all this is a serious matter, so we need to be straight up about everything cause this could affect a lot of people."

"Yeah, I gotcha," Raymond said, acknowledging Jamal's note of seriousness.

"I was checking out the news a few minutes ago and it came across the screen about the massacre that happened over on Vinewood. I'm saying, it ain't hard to tell that it's a drug war going on out there, and I need to know on the straight-up tip if you're involved in that in any way."

"If you ain't been out there it might be kind of hard for you to understand how it goes; I mean like the crew I'm down with ain't really beefing with none of them cats that's involved with that, but if they got people that got caught up in it they may want to retaliate. But I'm like Wes, I ain't in this mess.

"Now if I get drawn into it indirectly you'll be the first I'll let know. You might not know it, but a lot of dudes out there already know that you are out and they ain't too quick to try and get involved in no war with dudes like, you, Blood Lawson, Li'l Al, or none of them dudes that's been up the way and still holding their own. Blood Lawson came home and struck fear in a lot of these young dudes, so they really wouldn't want to go up against y'all unless they're pushed."

"Yeah, all that's good to know, but I'm not trying to be out there in no senseless war if I can help it. But if I have to go I'm going to go right. What kind of automatics can you get a hold of for me?" Jamal asked.

"Right now I can get a hold of TECH-9 MAC-10s, Aks, and a Glock," Raymond said.

"Okay, you handle that and I'm going to holler at my people about some explosives. I ain't messing around, if they bring it this way I'm going to blow some of these suckers off the map. I hope it don't come to that. You got to keep me posted, though, if you do get involved, so I'll have time to relocate your mama and the kids; whatever happens to us don't matter. I really don't want no beef with none of my people, but I ain't running from nothing, you know what I'm saying?"

Raymond knew that he could count on Jamal if something went down, but he didn't want to be the cause of getting him involved in anything that would send him back to prison. Plus, he knew his mother would never forgive him if he were to cause her brother to return to prison. She had already given up on Raymond, for she deemed it inevitable that he either would land in prison or catch an early burial.

of war. Jamal was on the phone beeping Byrd; he needed someone on a more professional level to discuss this with. Byrd had a lot of street contacts, and if he didn't already know what was going on, he could always find out.

He finally reached Byrd, and Byrd agreed to come pick him up; however, it would have to be after it had gotten dark. Byrd, for the most part, laid low, but he was also drama-prone; it didn't take much to draw him out of the cut if there was heavy drama going down. It didn't get dark until 8:00, and Jamal didn't want to be out too late as he had to get up in the morning for work. But when dealing with Byrd, he didn't have much choice, as Byrd, as a rule, didn't come out in the daytime for precautionary measures.

Jamal finished watching the news until Yolanda had dinner ready. They ate mostly in silence, everybody thinking their own thoughts about the massacre which had happened just a few streets over from where they lived. It carried a psychological impact on their family; knowing the possibility of Raymond being involved either directly or indirectly. For, after all, it was no secret that Raymond was in the drug game, and more than likely this was the beginning of a drug war. When everyone had finished eating, Yolanda motioned for Jamal to step in her room for a little private talk.

"Jamal, do you think that Raymond or some of his friends may be involved in this?"

"Well I couldn't say right now; that'll depend on if some of the people he connected to had friends or relatives in that house."

"And if they did, then what?"

"They would probably want to retaliate."

"Well we need to find out definitely before it's too late."

"I'm going to find that out this evening, so don't panic, I got this."

He left and went to his room to do some thinking until it became dark outside.

About a couple of hours later it began to get dark, and Jamal decided to wait on Byrd in the living room. He was so into his thoughts he wasn't even aware that Yolanda's boyfriend had shown up. He really didn't know him, but he had been introduced to him when he first came home. He was a little older than Jamal, about thirty-seven or thirty-eight, more of the clean-cut working type; he really didn't fit into the street crowd at all.

"My man! What's up?" Jamal spoke, acknowledging him.

"How's it going, Jamal?" He had heard about Jamal from Yolanda and the kids and from some of the people he worked with on his job before he even met him.

"I just been taking it easy," Jamal answered.

Right then a horn blew outside and Jamal knew it was Byrd.

"Oh! That's for me," Jamal said getting up from his chair, "I'm out y'all," He went out the door quickly, hoping no one would spot Byrd.

But it was too late. Yolanda looked out the window and spotted him, even though he changed rides. Jamal hopped in the car.

"Where to?" Byrd asked.

"The Cadillac."

There weren't many places Byrd could go without taking the chance of the wrong person spotting him.

"This must be kind of urgent?" Byrd stated.

"Yeah in a sense," Jamal said.

Byrd pulled into the motel's parking lot and drove toward the back so as to keep out of sight as much as possible. Once inside Byrd checked around as usual; however, not as much as before. He was obviously becoming more at ease with this cozy little room of Jamal's choosing. Finally satisfied, Byrd pulled out a pint of Crown Royal and some paper cups and poured Jamal and himself a drink.

"So what's up?" Byrd asked.

"Man, I need to find out what that shit was about last night over on Vinewood."

"You talking about the massacre?"

"Yeah, I'm trying to find out what it was about, who's at war, 'cause that was something big."

"Damn dog, you writing a book or something?" Byrd asked puzzled.

"Naw, what I'm really trying to find out is if my nephew or his crew is involved."

"Who he wit'?"

"I think the Y.K.2 boys," Jamal said, wondering if he was correct.

"You ain't got to worry then. That's Bunchy and them. They ain' wit' that, at least from what I heard. They talking like it was the Down River mob; some of they spots got hit and people thinking it was retaliation. I'll check it out though; me and Bunchy go back a few years, done a little business here and there."

"I'd appreciate it because if my nephew's in it, I might have to go."

"This is the kind of shit I was telling you about when you came home. The dope game is messed up, ain't no loyalty to that game, ain't no respect, and ain't no rules nobody going by. Your nephew is going to get caught up sooner or later if he ain't already caught up, I just hate to see you get dragged up in it."

"Yeah me too, that's the last thing I need," he said while his mind was still wandering. "Hey! You remember Gato the Mexican that was up North with us?" he asked Byrd.

"Oh yeah, you talking about the Mexican that was down with the revolutionary group that blew up them buildings across Eight Mile."

"Yeah, that's my man. You know somebody that can put me in touch with him?"

"Let me see. Oh yeah, Spanish Rob. I'll get a hold of him; he'll get you hooked up," Byrd said confidently.

"How long you think that'll take?" Jamal asked.

"Shouldn't be no more than a day," Byrd told him.

They drank and kicked it awhile until Byrd got up and said, "Man, I gotta bounce; you rollin'?"

"Naw. I'm going to chill, until the morning then go to work from here."

"Oh you gigging, huh?"

"Yeah, I got a maintenance job at a school on the Eastside D.T.I."

"Oh yeah, that's the school that Champ goes to. Got a lot of slick chicks and knucklehead jokers that go there."

"You get that right," Jamal agreed.

"Okay man, I'm out. I'll get back to you in about a day or so on that."

"All right Byrd, take it easy."

Byrd peeped out the window to see if the coast was clear, then left the same way he had came.

Jamal just leaned back in his chair and began to sort things out in his mind. He began thinking out loud. "Damn! I ain't been home a good month yet and 'bout to get caught up in some nonsense I ain't got nothing to do with."

All his plans would go down the drain if this crap was to go down, he thought to himself in silence again, but he must be prepared just the same. He couldn't leave his nephew hanging. Damn, why did that little fool have to be mixed up in the dope game? Then again he realized: in such an environment as this, along with the circumstances that surrounded him (no father figure around, kicked out of school, in and out of juvenile facilities, what else was he to do? The best thing he could do for his nephew if he was involved was to try to head this thing off before it grew into something that couldn't be stopped.

Jamal went to a pay phone to call Yolanda to let her know he would be leaving for work from the motel. Yolanda, curious as to why he didn't come home—especially after leaving with Byrd—said, "I hope you're not getting ready to do anything foolish with that maniac I saw you leave with."

"Come on now, every time you see me with him doesn't mean we're getting ready to do something. He's just a source where I get the valuable information from."

"I don't mean to make a big deal over it; he just gives me the creeps when he comes around," she said apologetically.

"Well you can rest at ease. He went back to the Eastside and I'm at a motel by myself. I'll see you tomorrow. Bye."

"Goodbye," she said.

It was around ten o'clock and he was feeling somewhat exhausted. He would take a shower and retire for the night.

Chapter 10

Jamal checked out of the motel at five-thirty the next morning. He went to a restaurant and ordered his breakfast. He began reading the newspaper he had gotten out of the newsstand in front of the restaurant. There were no clues yet in the Vinewood massacre and no suspects. The only thing the paper stated was that it was drug related. Six people had been slain in the house: four young black males and two young African-American females. Robbery was ruled out as a possible motive, as jewelry and money were still on the victims when found. All had been shot four times at close range, and there was no forced entry; obviously they had been set up by someone who was in the house and who let the assassins in.

Jamal finished his breakfast, paid for his meal, and went outside to hail a taxi. He arrived at the school around twenty minutes to seven. Catrina was already there; she greeted him vigorously.

"Good morning, Jamal. You certainly believe in getting to work on time."

"Oh, indeed, I've heard the early bird gets the worm," he said with a smile.

"You would definitely catch it coming out of its hole," she smiled back, looking over her shoulder as she went into the office.

He strolled down to the student lounge, hoping to overhear some gossip about what had happened on Vinewood Street. To his expectancy there were about five students sitting around the lounge drinking coffee and gossiping in general. He pulled a book out and began reading, while at the same time keeping his ears wide open for any discussion concerning the massacre. About five minutes later a young man came through the door hollering at the people sitting at the table.

"Yo!, Y'all hear about the drive-by that happened on the Westside up on Warner and Vinewood?"

"Quit all that hollering, fool," a young man at the table said.

"Oh my bad." They began to talk more in a whisper, yet they still could be heard.

"Hey! You talking about up at Big Tops?" one of the girls asked in a tone a little above a whisper. (Big Top was the party store where a lot of the local ballers from that neighborhood hung out drinking or just shooting the bull.)

"Yeah, in the parking lot," the young man said.

"They say who got hit?"

"Naw, they think it was Down River Boys or Y.K.2."

Jamal's heart skipped a beat. He got up and went downstairs to the phone booth to call Raymond, hoping to catch him before he got into the streets—if he even came home that night. The phone rang for a couple of minutes, still no answer; obviously no one was there. He hung up the receiver feeling somewhat agitated. He thought about beeping Byrd, but he hated to keep bothering him, yet there was no one else he could contact as of that moment, even though he knew Byrd didn't mind, as long as it was dark, as it gave him something to do. He knew it was risky for Byrd to travel across town, but as long as he took the freeway, he would much rather risk coming to you as there was a far greater risk in someone knowing his whereabouts. Finally, making up his mind, he beeped Byrd.

"Yo! What's up?" Byrd answered skeptically.

"It's Jamal."

"What's shaking, dog?"

"I need to holler at you again tonight; it's important."

"Ain't no problem, what time?"

"Nine o'clock. I'll be at that same spot, same room; if not I'll beep back."

"Solid," Byrd said and hung up.

Jamal had a big day in front of him. He was supposed to meet Cathy at six, Byrd at nine, and try to catch Raymond when he got off from work. He went back inside to attend to his chores. He worked up until lunchtime, then went across the street to the Burger King hoping to catch Champ again, as he hadn't seen him all that morning in the building. He ordered fish and fries and sat in the same booth he had sat in the day before. Champ came through the door around the same time. He was doing his internship in the mornings at a medical clinic and came to class in the afternoon, which is the reason Jamal had missed seeing him in the building that morning.

"Same table, huh?" Champ said.

"Yeah, you know, just like up the way in the chow hall. I ain't been able to shake them ways yet."

"Takes a little time," Champ said. "So how's the new job coming along?" he asked Jamal.

"It's all right you know, a job, ain't nothing to write back to the fellas about."

"Yeah picture that."

"Hey yo! You hear about that massacre on Vinewood?" Jamal asked.

"Yeah that's bad, puts a lot of heat on the game."

"They say there was another shooting last night up at Big Tops; you didn't hear about that?" Jamal said fishing.

"Naw, I don't get out much. I get everything on the tail end."

Jamal sensed that Champ was of no use in that area and dropped the subject. They engaged in their usual small talk and left for the school together. On their way there Jamal stopped by the phone booth to call Raymond to see if he could catch him at home. The phone rang for a few minutes, but no answer. It was rather difficult to catch Raymond, he sensed, especially if he was somehow involved in the events.

If this thing was going in the direction he thought it was, he soon would have to make a decision with Yolanda and the kids, either to move them to the suburbs to stay with his mother or into an apartment across town.

He busied himself through the rest of the day attending to the chores of the school rather quietly, his mind mostly preoccupied with the events in his neighborhood. People passed him in the hallway and some spoke, but most sensed that he was not too approachable if you didn't know him. So far his only conversation had been with Champ and a few mild words with Catrina.

It was nearing four o'clock, so he began wrapping things up, as he wanted to hurry and get back to the hood as soon as possible. He finally punched out and was headed for the stairs that would exit the school when Catrina spotted him and said, "You sure are in a hurry today," she hinted as though she wanted him to escort her out of the building.

"Yeah, I'm trying to catch my nephew before he darts off somewhere."

"Oh well, I'll see you tomorrow then."

"Okay, sure tang," he said, rushing down the steps.

As he walked toward the street to hail a taxi he thought to himself, *Maybe I'll escort her tomorrow if things don't get too hectic.* Then he quickly washed the thought out of his mind.

When he reached the house no one was there, so he decided to take a bath and tidy up a little so he wouldn't have to rush to meet Cathy. When he got through, he called a cab. Yolanda hadn't come home yet with the kids, and he didn't have time to wait on them. The cab arrived within the next fifteen minutes, so he decided first to go and rent a room at Cadillac—only this time he rented it for an entire weekend. He was fortunate enough to get the same room as before, so he didn't have to beep Byrd. He used the same cab to take him to the library downtown. It was a quarter to six when he arrived, so he did his usual and waited for Cathy on the library steps. He pulled a book out of his pocket and began to read. Instinctively he looked up and there it was, the white Cougar. She parked her car in the same spot, right in front of the library, and blew her horn. *Damn*, he thought. *Why does she always have to do that?* It was drawing attention; didn't she realize that everyone would spot him going to her car? After all, this was Detroit. Three black men were killed by white police officers for being with white women during the '67 riots in what then was called the Algiers Motel Incident. He hurried down the steps feeling that all eyes were on him. He opened the car door and hopped in rather horridly.

"My God! Someone after you?" she said.

"Naw, but let's get out of here. I'll explain to you later."

She sped off as if someone was chasing them.

"You can slow down; no one's after me."

"Well Jesus, I couldn't tell the way you came down those steps and jumped in the car."

He didn't realized he'd come down those steps as fast as he did.

"Where to?" she asked.

"We'll go to Greektown and have dinner," he strongly suggested.

When they arrived, he told her to find a parking space anywhere and they could walk from there, as he knew they would be less conspicuous in Greektown as an interracial couple. They walked to Tony's, going virtually unnoticed. They chose a booth near the rear once they were inside. A waitress came and handed them a menu; another came and poured the water. Cathy ordered peppered steak and Jamal ordered fried rice and garlic bread along with a bottle of dinner wine.

"Well, how'd it go the first couple of days on the job?" Cathy asked.

"The job is not bad, but the school is whack."

"Why do you say that?" she asked.

"Because first of all, the operators of the school are perpetrating a fraud, having no intentions of helping anybody. Its sole purpose is to play the students on their loan, knowing that over half will not graduate and only a handful will obtain a job as a result of graduating. The longer it takes to pay back the loan, the more the interest piles up, and it's all coming off the backs of poor black folks," Jamal stated emphatically.

"Wow! You figured all that out in a day?"

"In my dialectical studies, I've learned to penetrate the veil of appearance from the door. That which appears on the surface is not necessarily so; one must check beneath it in order to get to the essence. Most people are fooled by appearance."

"Maybe that's exactly what I've done," she said.

"What's that?" he asked.

"Judged the school and a lot of other things on face value—a common mistake a lot of us make."

"I wouldn't call it a mistake," He said.

"You wouldn't?"

"No, because the educational system we live under trains us to accept things without investigation. That's why a whole lot of American people are easily misled, blinded by appearances, which makes them easy prey to be ruled by way of deception," Jamal elaborated.

Cathy, in deep thought, realized with all the education she had she was nowhere near enlightened to the ways of the world as this man from the streets was with little education from the academic world. Switching the subject Cathy asked, "Wasn't that in your neighborhood where six people were slain in the house?"

"Yeah a few streets over, as a matter of fact."

"You are living in a dangerous neighborhood, aren't you?"

"Well the condition we live under makes it dangerous."

"How's that?" she asked curiously.

"Any time you have a poor neighborhood with people out of work and who can't find employment while at the same time promoting luxury as a nation's aspiration, yet failing to provide a means to obtain it. You have already created a dangerous situation. And on top of that you do nothing to halt the flood of drugs in that community where weapons are made so accessible; you have just set the stage for a ghetto war."

"Well since you know all this, can't you make the people aware so they won't fall into the trap?" she asked, earnestly wanting to know.

"You take five hungry dogs who haven't eaten in three or four days and throw a bone in their midst and see if you can keep them from attacking one another over it," he illustrated.

He certainly has a way of putting things to make his point, she thought to herself.

"So basically there isn't much anyone can do, right? I said, *there isn't much anyone can do?*" she said in a louder voice.

"Oh naw, naw," he said, snapping out of a zone. He had drifted off thinking about Raymond's situation.

"Is something the matter?" Cathy asked, disturbed.

"Huh! Oh naw, I'm all right. I was just thinking about something."

"What were you thinking about? You can tell me," she asked.

Damn, he thought to himself, *what the hell is she? A psychologist now?* Well he thought maybe he'd better tell her something he figured out because it would be hard to keep his mind off his nephew's situation and talk to her about something else at the sametime.

"It's my nephew, really. It's not that he's involved in anything himself, but some of the people he's connected with may be involved in something that could affect his life as well as our family."

"How would it affect you family?" she seemed not to understand.

"Well, the way some of these fools out here think, if they can't get you, they try to get those close to you."

"That's not fair," she reasoned.

"Nothing's fair in love and war," he quoted.

My goodness, she thought, *this will be more than just getting a glimpse at life in the ghetto streets*. She actually felt as though she was involved to a certain degree by committing herself to help this man she had come to grow so fond of. It was exciting on the one hand, but could become dangerous on the other.

"What do you plan to do?" she asked.

"First I'll find out tonight what's what, then if he is involved directly or indirectly, I'll have to relocate Yolanda and the kids. The next step is to see if his life is in any way threatened; if so I may have to come to his aid."

"But you don't have anything to do with that?"

"You're right about that, but I can't stand by and let one of these idiots put a bullet in him and not lift a finger. I'd feel less than a man."

"That could risk everything you set out to do."

"Yeah, I know. That's why I was telling you on the bus, in my world there are no long-range plans."

"Well let's hope that it doesn't come to that. You haven't even had a chance to experience life yet."

Damn, she got me going down if it does jump, he said to himself. But he figured it wise to fill her in to some degree, just in case things got ugly and he had to put a few people in the ground. She would be able to come to his defense, at least character-wise. There was nothing like having the rich and white go to bat for you when dealing with the criminal justice system.

It was about seven-thirty and would be getting dark soon and he wanted to make a quick run by the house to see if he would be able to catch Raymond. They finished their meal in silence and strolled to the parking lot. She took him by the house, and the car was in the driveway. That meant either Raymond was inside or he had left with some of his friends.

He told Cathy to wait in the car; he would be right back. He didn't have time to be introducing her to everybody. He went inside and everyone was there except Raymond.

"Has Raymond been here?" he asked Yolanda.

"Yes, he was here for a minute then left with a couple of his little thug friends. Why?"

"He was supposed to pick up something important for me."

She wasn't stupid. She knew it had to be a gun—what else would he be picking up for him with all this crazy nonsense going on? However, she knew, whatever was on his mind, she wouldn't be able to stop him at this point. His mind was more than likely already made up.

"Well he didn't leave any messages for you."

"That's all right, I'll catch him later. I'm going to be at that motel again for tonight and leave for work from there in the morning."

"Did you find out anything yet?" she asked.

"Not yet, that's what I'm going to do now; see you later," he said as he went out the door.

Yolanda saw him get in the car with Cathy and was relieved that it wasn't Byrd. Cathy drove him to the motel. When they arrived she asked him if she could come in and use the bathroom. He had no problem with that as Byrd wasn't due until nine o'clock and it wasn't even eight o'clock yet. He thought to himself, *She really does trust me.* However, he was worried whether anyone would notice them. The key thing that was in his favor was that the motel was situated in a secluded area. As they entered the room, Cathy, more muttering to herself, said, "What a cozy little place this is," then pointed toward the back.

"That must be the bathroom over there."

"Yeah, everything else is right out here."

She took about ten minutes; it was five past eight when she came out. She felt quite comfortable being with him in the little amount of time that they knew each other. He was not a bad person in her eyes just serious about the things he was about and maybe took them to the extreme; outside of that she felt she could trust him.

"Why are you staying here?" She seemed to be curious.

"More privacy and seclusion. I can get a lot more done, plus I have a few people dropping by that aren't too acceptable other places."

She wondered what he meant by that but didn't want to appear nosy.

"Have a seat. We have a few minutes before I have to take care of some things," he offered.

She sat in the chair at the desk and crossed her legs. *Damn, why did she have to do that?* he thought to himself as her skirt hiked up a couple more inches; he tried to restrain himself from looking down at her legs.

"I assume you have quite a few women visitors dropping by?"

What the hell was she trying to imply? Now he wished he had never invited her to sit and talk; she made him nervous.

"You assumed wrong. I don't even know any woman at the present outside of you," he said with a slight smile.

"Oh, I keep forgetting—you've been out of commission for over a decade."

"That's right, thanks for reminding me."

"Jamal, I do hope you don't get mixed up in this thing with your nephew."

"All I can do is promise you I'm going to try everything I can not to."

She looked at her watch. "Well, it's getting late; I have to be getting back. When can we get together again? I'd like to go to the library with you so you can introduce me to the real world of study."

"How about this weekend, say uh . . . Saturday afternoon about twelve-thirty?"

"Okay, that'll be fine. Do you want me to meet you there?"

"Yeah, I'll be there; if anything changes I'll let you know."

"All right, see you then."

"Wait. I'll walk you to your car; we're in carjacking territory."

He grabbed his jacket with the .45 inside and put it on just in case they ran into some fools. As soon as they got to her car two young men were approaching them. Jamal had spotted them coming from a distance and already had his gun by his side concealed to a certain degree. The young men sensed that they might have a problem with him and decided just to ask a question.

"Is this the only motel around here?"

"Yeah, it's the only one I know about," Jamal answered, demonstrating no fear.

The young man on the left spotted the pistol in Jamal's hand and nudged his partner, signaling him to get up outta there. They moved on without incident.

"Wow! That was a close call. Do you think they were going to try and take the car?"

"You never can tell out here on these streets," he said.

"I didn't know you carried a gun."

"I don't carry one. I just keep it on hand for situations like this—which probably just saved you the loss of your car and probably your life."

"I can't argue with that," she said, getting into the car.

"You should be safe from here; stay on the streets that are lit up," he cautioned her.

"All right, take care," she said as she drove off into the night.

She took Michigan Avenue to the freeway so she had nothing to worry about. This was all very exciting to her—a new experience indeed. She had never been to any place where it wasn't safe to enter certain areas at night, where you had to worry about getting your car jacked, people getting slain a couple of streets over, or the people you were involved with carrying guns; or where a riot may break out at any moment or a drug war was going on right around the corner. All this was occurring just a few days after meeting one individual.

She had driven all the way home before she discovered she had left her purse in the bathroom at the motel. She had never paid any attention to the name of the motel, but she knew where it was located and would have to go all the way back to get it. It was almost nine o'clock. She rested a minute, then fixed herself a cup of tea and decided to drive back to the motel to retrieve her purse.

Byrd showed up at the motel a little after nine. He parked in the back of the motel as usual, then checked around to see if anyone was out and about—especially any cops. After he felt everything was okay he slid up the back way. Jamal let him in and Byrd did his usual checking around. He noticed the purse in the bathroom and smiled, as he assumed Jamal had came across him a little leg on his own. After Byrd checked under the bed, he put his pistol up and pulled out a pint of Martel and two cups. Jamal wasn't much of a drinker, only to be sociable, but he sure could use one now, he felt.

Byrd set the cups on the table, poured the drinks, kicked back on the bed, and said, "What's shaking?"

"Man, there was a driveby up on warren at Top's I don't know how many people got hurt, but I heard it could have been Y.K.2 or Down River Mob that got rocked."

"Yeah, one died and two was injured, I did some checking up and found out that Y.K.2. joined forces with Twenty Grand Boys against the Down River Mob. It could get ugly," Byrd theorized.

Suddenly there was a knock at the door. Byrd pulled his pistol and whispered, "Feds."

"Who is it?" Jamal hollered.

"It's me, Cathy; I think I left my purse in the bathroom"

Jamal motioned to Byrd to put the gun away. Byrd hesitated then put it away reluctantly.

Jamal opened the door, and Cathy almost choked as she looked directly into the eyes of Byrd.

"Oh excuse me. I didn't know you had company."

"That's Frank, a friend of mine."

Byrd nodded his head in acknowledgment. Cathy, still somewhat spooked at Byrd's appearance, avoided his eyes as he had the look of a killer.

"I hadn't even looked in the bathroom." Jamal said, trying to relieve some of the tension in the room.

"I'm pretty sure that's where I left it."

"Yeah, I peeped it; it's still in there," Byrd comment trying to put Cathy at ease. Jamal went to the bathroom and came back with it in his hand. "Is this it?"

"Yes, thank you." She saw that everything was just as it was when she left it.

"I hate that you had to come all the way back here," Jamal said.

"I didn't realize it until I had gotten home."

"Is everything there?" Jamal asked.

"Oh yes, just like I left it."

"Would you care for a drink? Looks like you've had a pretty rough day," Byrd offered.

"Oh no thank you, I better be getting back; it's getting late."

"I'll escort you back to your car," Jamal said, assuring her safety.

"Yeah, you better do that," Byrd said, trying to set her at ease as much as possible.

"Well it was nice meeting you, Frank."

"My pleasure," Byrd said courteously.

As soon as Jamal and Cathy left the room Byrd pulled out his pistol, still suspicious of Cathy, thinking she could be working undercover. He cracked the door to make sure he could hear any unusual sounds if there were any. He went to the window to watch her leave and felt a little more comfortable once he saw her pull off, as he didn't trust white folks, no matter what the circumstances were; to him they were all either the police or working for them.

He heard one set of footsteps coming up the stairs and figured it to be Jamal. Anyway, he was never worried about any one man, be he police or not, as he always kept the edge.

On her way home Cathy was worried about Jamal. He must be involved in some type of way to be in the company of someone like Frank, she thought. She was 100 percent sure that Frank was a killer; it was written all over him.

Back at the Motel, Jamal was trying to convince Byrd that Cathy was straight up and not affiliated with any law agency. He told him how he had met her on the bus coming home from prison and that she had helped him get a job and that their relationship extended no further than platonic. Byrd calmed down a bit and was now back on business.

"I got a hold of Spanish Rob, and he gave me Gato's hook-up."

Byrd reached into his pocket and grabbed a slip of paper and handed it to Jamal. It had Gato's address and beeper number on it, along with his home phone.

"When is the last time you saw Li'l Al?" he asked Byrd.

"Let's see, it must have been about three weeks ago on some business he had lined up. Li'l Al is on some extortion shit; he got a crew of young killers he's using to extort some of them big dope boys who ain't got no heart. Now I hear he's trying to extort some top-notch rappers. That fool better slow down before they roast his ass."

"Yeah, well I might need him. You think you can get a hold of him and arrange a meeting with me and him?"

"Yeah, aint no problem. That's my man, and even though that little beef y'all had up the way kind of distanced y'all, he still got a lot of love for you."

"I want him to know that's behind us, and we can come together on mutual terms."

"Yeah I'll take care of that," Byrd said.

"I might need you and Blood on this one, too; the next one's on me."

"Oh yeah, you know you got that coming on the strength. Besides, them jokers is poot butts, take down a couple of them that suppose to be like that and the rest'll fold," Byrd said with confidence.

"Okay, I'll get back with you as soon as I find out how things are laying."

"Awight, just give me a beep." Byrd left the same way he came.

Jamal would contact Gato tomorrow to see what he could get in terms of explosives. If it was going down he was going to take it to another level. It was about ten o'clock. Tomorrow was Friday, and he had a big week coming up starting after work. He took a quick shower and retired for the night.

Chapter 11

The next morning Jamal went to the restaurant across the street from the motel. He grabbed a newspaper from the stand to see if anything else had happened. There was an article about the driveby that occurred on Warren Avenue in the parking lot of the party store, where one person was killed and several wounded in what the police department believed was in some way connected to the Vinewood massacre; still no suspects in either incident. Jamal knew that the city didn't really care as long as it was black-on-black crime. But since there were so many killed in one incident, they would be forced to pin the murder on someone sooner or later, as the community put pressure on the department to get those murders solved.

Jamal knew how people in the streets acted and reacted. Tonight being Friday, with so many people out and about, there was certain to be some killings connected to the Vinewood incident. He just hoped he could reach Raymond before the boy got himself involved in something bigger than he realized. Detroit is a dangerous city when it comes to killing as it was the first city to earn the name the "murder capital." This thing could blow way out of proportion if somebody didn't put a cap on it.

He finished his meal and went outside to hail a taxi to take him to work. When he arrived at the school he didn't see Catrina, so he punched in and went to the student lounge to see if he could come across some information. He saw one of the younger men that was conducting the drug transaction in the bathroom a few days ago. He wanted to ask him a few questions but thought better of it, as he realized that most of the young cats were crowd-pleasers and might say the wrong thing out of their mouth, forcing him into a situation where he might have to react violently. That was the worst thing he needed at the present.

One thing Jamal noticed was that he wouldn't be picking up anything from that individual anyway, as he always seemed to be talking in a whisper. The one thing Jamal didn't do was listen in on others' conversations; you just had to be talking loud enough for the whole room to hear you in order for him to pick up anything. There wasn't much talk in the open about anything of any significance to him, so he left to attend to his chores. On the way down the hall he met Catrina coming his way.

"Late getting in this morning, I see."

"Yeah, those darn kids waited all the way until Friday to start fooling around before school."

"I didn't know you were married," he stated, hoping he was wrong.

"I'm not. Well at least not anymore; me and that fool broke up years ago."

"How many young'ns you got?"

"Just two, and they're driving me crazy," she said.

"I guess you ain't trying to have anymore then, huh?"

""Not right now. I can't afford it," she said; however that left room open for the future.

"I imagine so if you haven't got a man to share the cost with."

"That's one of the primary problems, finding a good man."

"Yeah, I know what you mean," Jamal said as she was stepping off.

He worked up until his break time and went to the phone booth to call Gato; he dialed his home number. The phone rang and a voice came through the other end.

"Hola! Ouien es?"

"Soy yo Jamal."

"Hey! Como esta?"

"Bien," Jamal answered in Spanish. He could speak a little Spanish but understood it well.

"What you been up to, man?" Gato asked him.

"I just got out a couple of weeks ago, and I need a favor."

"Sure man, you know, if I can help."

"You remember what we use to talk about when we was in the hole?"

"Oh yeah!" he said.

"Well, I'm going to need some of that."

"I see, I see. Give me a number where I can contact you, and as soon as I can get that together I'll buzz you."

"Gracias." He gave Gato his home number.

"If I'm not there, leave a message."

"Gotcha! Te veo," Gato said and hung up.

Now that Jamal had gotten all that out of the way, he needed to try to catch Raymond. He tried calling but got no answer. If he could get in touch with Li'l Al he would be able to track Raymond down through some of the young guys that were working under Li'l Al. They all seemed to know each other or about each other, regardless of what crew they were down with.

Jamal went back to work until lunchtime. He made his way over to the Burger King for lunch and noticed there were a few more people in there than usual, probably because it was Friday, when the crowd liked to gather in order to make their weekend plans. He really didn't see anyone he actually knew whom he had anything in common with; most were just ordinary working-class people who had been out of work and couldn't find employment. They either liked to party, get high, or go clubbing or to other events of entertainment. There were maybe two or three who peddled their drugs to the students. He did spot one of them whom he assumed was a drug boy, and they had spoken to each other on occasion, so he figured he might as well try to see if the little fellow knew his nephew.

"Yo young-blood! Let me holler at you a minute."

"Yeah, what's up, dog?" he said as he slid into the booth where Jamal was seated. Normally he would have asked "what you need," referring to drugs, but he could tell from Jamal's demeanor that he wasn't looking for any drugs.

"Man, I been trying to locate my nephew since I've been out of the joint. I heard he was down with Y.K.2., but damn, I don't know none of them either."

"Well right now it might be kind of hard to catch up with him."

"Why is that?" Jamal asked.

"'Cause they done got in the middle of that Vinewood massacre thing."

"How they do that?"

"Joining up with Fifty Grand."

"You know a little dude named Raymond, kind of heavy-set, light skinned, with a low-cut fade?" Jamal asked.

"Oh yeah, now I remember you—the dude they snatched for starting the riot. Yeah I know Raymond, but I ain't seen him in a while."

"You know where he hangs at?"

"Yeah, sometimes he hangs at Charley's or up at the Rainbow."

"Awight dog, good looking." Jamal thanked him.

"Hey, so You his uncle, huh?"

"Yeah that's me."

"I'll be seeing you around. Take it easy. I'm out."

"Awright, do the same," Jamal reciprocated.

After he finished eating Jamal went to the phone booth again. This time he beeped Byrd. He waited for the phone to ring. He picked up the receiver and the voice on the other end said skeptically, "Who's that?"

"Jamal."

"Oh what's up? I'm glad you beeped; I got you lined up with Li'l Al for tonight."

"Good, where we going to meet?" Jamal asked.

"You still got that room at the motel?"

"Yeah, I booked it for the whole weekend."

"Okay, we'll be by about 8:30."

"Awright, bet," Jamal said hanging up the phone.

Things were beginning to fall into place now. If he could just catch Raymond, he thought. He figured if he couldn't catch him at home, he would try those places the youngster told him about. He tried calling the house again; still no answer. He would try again on his next break. He went back to the school building to finish cleaning the offices as was required on Fridays.

Chapter 12

Raymond had gotten the guns for Jamal, an AK-47 and a TECK-9. The beef with the Down River Mob had escalated as one of the Y.K.2. boys had been gunned down in the park assumedly by the Down River mob for joining forces with the 20 Grand crew. It was getting to the point now where anybody who got caught off guard or was in the wrong territory was a target.

   Raymond was hesitant about telling Jamal because he didn't want him to get involved, but at the same time he didn't want to put his family in jeopardy. He decided he must tell Jamal soon before things went to the next level—the indiscriminate killing—where friends, family, and anyone associated with either side was vulnerable. He also knew that he was subject to be called upon to move on a member of the Down River mob; it was just a matter of time. He took the guns home and stashed them in his room in case the house got raided. He knew enough about the law that if his uncle, an ex-felon, got pinned for the guns he wouldn't see day light for awhile. He himself would get off a lot lighter, so naturally he would take the weight for them. Just as he was fixing himself something to eat the phone rang, and he snatched up the receiver.

   "What's up? Who is this?"

   "Jamal!"

   "Oh what's up, Jamal?"

   "Man, I been trying to catch you for two days."

   "I been busy, dog; I got that what you ask for."

   "Awright, my man, where you going to be at when I get off work?"

   "What time you get off?"

   "Four o'clock."

"Okay I'll drop back by here around four-thirty. If you're not here I'll wait on you."

"Yeah, that'll work. Check you then."

"Aight, see ya," Raymond said as he hung the phone up.

Jamal sensed Raymond's desperation. He knew that he would now have to go to war with these fools; there was no getting around it. Yeah, he could send Raymond off somewhere—the thought had passed through his mind—but they grew up in that neighborhood; to run from a fight would be a shameful act no matter what the circumstances were. The family name was far more important, he reasoned.

A lot rested on his alliance with Li'l Al, who had the resources to help him fight this battle the way it's supposed to be fought. He would recruit Byrd and Blood for the psychological impact it would carry, for once the Down River Mob realized that they were going up against real killers with a diehard mentality and also versed in the art of street war, they would lean toward some type of negotiation rather than risk their little empire crumbling, Jamal surmised. As Jamal cleaned the last office, which was Mr. Johnson's, Catrina appeared in the doorway.

"You're doing an excellent job on these offices."

"Yeah, well you know, I try to keep them looking sharp, gives the appearance of professionalism."

"I can't help but notice that you always seem to be in a hurry near the end of the day. Do you have another job that you have to go to when you leave here?" she asked.

He had to think quickly; he wanted to lie and say he did, as no explanation would be required for his hurried disposition, but he thought better and just told her he had some serious business to attend to. She knew little about him and could not quite figure him out; she just didn't know what it was. He definitely carried himself with confidence in everything that he did. He never was impolite or vulgar, but she also sensed a certain coldness about him that didn't allow one to get close to him.

"Well maybe one of these days when you settle down a bit I may be able to get you to escort me to my car," she told him.

"I might just take you up on that starting next week."

"Yeah, I'll bet," she said as she strolled off.

Man! he thought. *Why does all this crazy nonsense have to be happening at this particular time?* It seemed to be preventing him from living a normal life, something he hadn't been able to do in the past thirteen year. But that's life, he reasoned.

After he finished cleaning Mr. Johnson's office it was about three-thirty. Since there was nothing left to do, he punched out early, as he wanted to be sure to catch Raymond before one of those fools caught him. Plus, he had a big night ahead of him. When he reached the house, Raymond was there waiting for him. They greeted each other with a handshake and a hug.

"I got that for you, but I couldn't get the Glock Right now."

"So you got the TEC and the AK?"

"Yeah, c'mon, they're in my room."

Raymond opened the door to the closet where he had them stashed under a pile of clothes. When he pulled them out Jamal's eyes lit up like Christmas trees, as he had a fascination with guns. He took the AK first, broke it down, then nodded his approval to Raymond. He checked out the TEC and also nodded his approval.

"Not bad," he said.

"I should be able to get the GLOCK in a couple of days," Raymond assured him.

"So what you think, man? We going to have to use this stuff or what?" Jamal slid the question in.

"Well, from the way it's looking now I think it's best to have them."

Jamal made his decision right then.

"We can't afford to take no chances. I'm going to move your mama and the kids up outta here."

"Where they gon' go?" Raymond asked.

"I'll probably send them out there with your grandmother."

"Ah man! She gon' trip if she find out why they coming out there."

"Don't worry about that, I'll handle her," Jamal said with confidence.

"I hate this had to happen, you know, getting you involved and having to move the family."

"All that comes with the dope game. Most of the young cats don't think about that when they step into the game; all they looking at is the money. But they soon come to learn that ain't nothing in life free and then it's too late. That's why a lot of them break down and flip when they get busted, never even considered the consequences," Jamal preached.

"Yeah, I never thought it was going to come to all this. All I wanted to do was make a little change like everybody else," Raymond said with regret, realizing the gravity of the situation.

"Well it's on now, we got to do what we gotta do. I just hope you learn something from all this."

"I'm learning now," he said.

"Good, so what's the latest?"

"The Down River Mob gunned down Smokey in the park, so Y.K.2. is planning a retaliation move."

"Awright, so the stage is being set for open warfare."

"Yeah it kinda looks that way," Raymond said.

"Okay, I'm going to get with my people and set up shop, and the first sign that I see that it's no, I'm going into action and ain't nobody going to know where it's coming from, you know what I'm saying?"

"Yeah I feel ya, but you ain't been out there; how you going to know when it's time?"

"I got some people on it that'll know before you do."

"Okay then, I gots to bounce; I'll get back witcha."

"Awright stay tight," Jamal said as Raymond left out the door.

Jamal called his mother who lived in Inkster (a small suburb of Detroit comprised virtually of African-Americans) to see if Yolanda and the kids could come out there and stay with her awhile.

She would be glad to have them keep her company, as long as she knew nothing of the circumstances that brought them there. He told her they wanted to move out of the neighborhood and weren't yet able to find a neighborhood suitable for them. His mother agreed without question, something very unusual for her. He would take them out there in the morning, giving them the rest of the day and night to pack their things.

He put the T.V. on the news channel before the kids came home. Nothing had happened yet in regard to the drug war that was developing. There were still no suspects in the Vinewood massacre, so he turned to the world news and waited for Yolanda and the kids to get home.

They were talking about the situation in Iraq when Jamal heard the car pull up in the driveway. The only problem he could see that Yolanda and the kids would have about living out there with his mother is that everyone would have to get up a little earlier in order to make it to school and work on time.

"Hi Jamal," the kids spoke to him as they came through the door.

When Yolanda came in she said, "Well look who's home for a change."

"C'mon now, you know I been taking care of a lot of business."

"Well that you have," Yolanda said half jokingly.

"In fact, I called Mama and arranged for you and the kids to go out there and stay for a while until the situation with Raymond is nipped in the bud."

"So as of now things have gotten to that point?" she asked curiously.

"Yeah, it kinda looks that way; so to be on the safe side, I think it best that you and the kids go out there for now. And, oh yeah, don't let Mama know nothing about what's going on with Raymond."

"You know she's kind of nosy; she's going to want to know why we're coming out there all of a sudden," Yolanda stated.

"Just tell her the neighborhood is getting crazy and we're looking for a house somewhere else in the meantime.

"What time are we going out there?" she asked.

"Early, about nine o'clock, so you need to start packing after dinner. Just pack the stuff you need f'right now; don't worry about too much else," he said.

"Oh, I'm not, you can believe I have insurance on everything after living in this neighborhood for so long."

"I bet you have," Jamal said, agreeing.

"Red! Poochie! Wanda! Start packing your stuff; we're moving out to Grandma's house in the morning."

"Who said?" Poochie asked with defiance.

"Boy! I said, that's who said; now get that stuff packed," Yolanda screamed.

"What are you going to do?" she asked Jamal.

"I'll probably stay at the motel and keep checking by the house, but I'm going to need the car. I'll drive y'all out there, so that way Mama will have to let you use one of her cars."

"So that means you may be getting involved?" she asked, fishing.

"Yeah, well you know. I got to do what I got to do to protect your son," he said.

"That boy is hard headed; he's never going to learn."

"Hopefully this'll teach him a lesson."

"I doubt it," she said as she left and went into the kitchen.

The phone rang and Jamal answered it; it was Gato.

"Que pasa?" Gato spoke in Spanish.

"Pasa nada, what's up?" Jamal broke off the Spanish and spoke English.

"I got that, homes."

"Oh yeah, what time you want me to come pick it up?"

"Any time you're ready."

"Okay, I'll be right over," Jamal said, speaking in a rush.

"Te veo," Gato said, hanging up.

Gato didn't live too far from him; he lived in the neighborhood where Jamal went to school. The school was set in the middle of the Spanish neighborhood about a mile and a half from where Jamal lived.

"Yolanda, let me see your keys; I got to make a quick run."

"They're on the dresser."

Jamal arrived at Gato's and pulled all the way up in the driveway into the garage as was instructed. Gato was in the garage. When Jamal got out of the car they greeted and hugged each other as they had gotten real close after doing a year in solitary confinement together in the joint.

"Man, this is some high-powered stuff. Let me show you what I got."

He opened a black duffle bag and took everything out and put it on a rug. There were five hand grenades, four sticks of dynamite, four homemade pipe bombs, and some plastic explosives. Jamal knew how to work most of them except the plastic explosives. Gato instructed him on how to use them, then carefully placed them back into the duffle bag.

"Awright Gato, good looking, you know I gotcha."

"No problem, homes," Gato said.

"Te veo," Jamal said in Spanish as he backed out of the driveway.

When he got home he came in the house and went straight to his bedroom with the duffle bag. Yolanda saw him come in and figured he had gone to pick up some guns, but it was useless for her to say anything as she knew his mind was already made up.

"Your dinner's ready, Jamal."

He ate alone as she was busy packing her things. While he was eating he was contemplating whether to take the guns and explosives to the motel with him or leave them at the house. If he took them with him he ran the risk of getting stopped by the police and knew that he would be forced to use them, as there was no doubt about it—if he was to get caught with all of that, they would bury him in prison for life for sure. If he left them in the house, he ran the risk of those fools burning the house down in their pursuit of Raymond. It was a tough decision to make; however, he was always taught that it was better to be caught with the gun than without it. And since he carried the .45 with him he figured he might as well carry the whole load. He would wait until it started getting dark before he moved with the guns and explosives—less chances of being spotted, he concluded.

He told Yolanda that he needed to use the car again tonight to make a few runs, and if she wasn't planning on using it he would be back in the morning to take them to Inkster. Even if she didn't want to, for his sake she never denied him anything of hers. He went to his room and studied until around eight o'clock, then he decided to make his move. He put the guns in a suitcase and carried them in one hand and carried the duffle bag in another to give the appearance that he was moving, too, in case anybody just happened to be looking out of their windows.

He drove to the motel, taking all the streets that were lit up so as not to run into any stray bullets. When he arrived at the motel he carried the suitcase and the duffle bag the same way so if anybody saw him they would think he just got into town. When he reached his room he put the suitcase by the bed and the duffle bag under it.

It was nearing eight-thirty so he turned the T.V. on the news to see if he could catch anything before Byrd and Li'l Al showed up. It wasn't really late enough for anything big to happen yet. There were so many shootings in Detroit, especially on the weekend, that it would be impossible to report them all on the news. So only the ones that they felt merited attention got reported. There were more on the Eastside than in all the rest of the areas put together. The Eastside as a whole was the poorest and the roughest part of town in the city. However, there were certain sections on the Westside, such as The Pit where Jamal lived, that were equally as poor and rough; the same was the case with the Northend, where Byrd was from. As Jamal was changing the channel on the T.V. there was a knock on the door.

"Yeah, who is it," Jamal asked, fingering the .45 as he spoke.

"Byrd and Al," came the reply.

He opened the door and there stood a little fellow, about five foot five and a half or five six, with long hair pushed back in a ponytail and a neatly trimmed mustache, that gave him a distinct look.

"Yo! What's up, my brother?" Li'l Al said, extending his arms out to Jamal.

"It's been a while," Jamal said as they embraced each other.

Then Byrd and Jamal shook hands with a light hug.

"Y'all have a seat and get comfortable while I make us some drinks."

He had stopped by the liquor store and bought a fifth of rum and a six-pack of Coke. He broke out the cups and let everybody mix their own drinks.

"So how you been making it?" Jamal asked Li'l Al.

"All I do is stack and collect, ain't nothing out here on these streets but a bunch of fake wannabe gangsters; most of the real cats are locked down. I got a crew of young killers, top-of-the-line in the city. They ain't faking; they go on real missions, and they know how to keep their mouths shut."

"Sounds like you got it going on for real," Jamal commented.

"Just a little something something," he said and then added, "I heard you might be caught up in that little war that's about to come down."

"Yeah, that's what I needed to holler at you about."

"Run it," Al said.

"You know I'm kind of fresh out here on these streets and really don't know what's poppin'. I been gone too long, so I need you to keep me posted on what's what, and I may need you and your crew to hold me down if I have to step out there on behalf of my nephew."

"Man, that ain't no problem. You know how we do it; ain't nothing change. All you got to do is holla, and we'll put it in motion," Li'l Al said with confidence.

"What you gonna do? Wait 'til they move on your nephew?" Byrd interjected.

"Naw, as soon as I see that it's getting to the point where anybody's up for grabs, then it's time to move in and lay the lick down. You know what I'm saying; I don't want to be the one to open it up for that."

"Yeah, I feel ya; it's your call, man," Byrd surrendered.

"I figure by Sunday or Monday I should know how things stand. If anything jumps before then I'll give you a beep," he told Byrd.

"I'll give you a call tomorrow around this same time and post you up on the latest," Li'l Al told him as he was getting up to leave.

They all gave each other the fist touch, and Byrd and Li'l Al left the way they had come. Jamal kicked back in his chair, sipped from his drink, and tried to put things in perspective. The one thing he understood, if this thing went down the way he figured and he did get involved, he would be putting everything on the line: his job, his little bit of freedom, the cause for which he stood, in fact his whole life. Cathy was right about what she said: He really had not really lived yet, but then again, what had life meant to him but years of confinement, a constant struggle to survive, always on the bottom, ruled by another race of people, powerless at the hands of these ruthless people who governed his life? If he died today, tomorrow, or the next day, what the hell difference did it make? No one would lose or benefit from it. Life in his situation was meaningless.

The only thing he lived for anyway was to help try to liberate his people, a people who never experienced freedom, who had no concept of freedom and therefore were hard to push in the direction of liberation. Now he had to go fight a war that was taking him away from his real task, just to try to save his nephew's butt, who had jumped into a game with no awareness of who orchestrated it.

Little did he know it was for purposes for his own destruction.

With such powerful thoughts coupled with the few drinks he had, he fell fast asleep.

Chapter 13

Jamal woke up out of a deep sleep. As he awakened he panicked, as he had no idea of how much time had elapsed since he'd fallen asleep. He looked at his watch; it was 6:45 A.M. He hadn't expected to sleep that long, and it seemed as if he had slept for days. He must focus, he told himself. "Oh yeah," he said as he remembered he was supposed to take Yolanda and the kids out to his mother's house at nine o'clock, then he was supposed to meet Cathy at the library at twelve-thirty, and there was something else but it wasn't coming into focus. He thought for a minute; what the hell was it? Oh yeah, Li'l Al was going to get in touch with him that evening around eight-thirty to keep him posted on what was going on.

He would go to the restaurant across the street from the motel and eat breakfast and pick up a newspaper on the way to see if anything big happened the previous night. He took a seat in one of the booths in the restaurant and ordered his meal then opened the newspaper. There was nothing big as far as homicides on the front pages and only a couple of small incidents throughout the whole paper, which relieved him to a certain degree; at least he had time to take care of the things he needed to take care of.

After he finished eating his meal and reading the paper it was about twenty minutes to eight. He paid for the meal and went back to the motel. He had to figure out whether to leave the guns and explosives in the motel or take them back to the house. He couldn't take any couple of small incidents throughout the whole paper, which relieved chances; the maid would be cleaning up sometime that morning, so it would be better if he took them back to the house for now.

He looked at his watch; it was almost eight o'clock. He grabbed the suitcase and duffle bag and locked the door. If people saw him they would figure he had just gotten into town. He pulled up in the driveway at the house on Twenty-third. The screen door was the only door closed; you could see into the house. The kids were up running about and Yolanda had her bags packed by the door.

As he came through the door Red greeted him. "We ready, Jamal."
"Yeah, I can see that. Where's your mama?"
"Is that you, Jamal?" Yolanda hollered from the bathroom.
"Yeah it's me," he said.
"I'll be out in a minute," she hollered out.
"Awright."

Jamal took the suitcase and duffle bag to his bedroom and put it in a spot where he would have quick access if something happened. When he came out of the room Yolanda was dressed and ready to go.

"Is everybody ready?" Yolanda asked in general.
"Yeah, yeah," the kids hollered.
"Have you eaten already?" she asked Jamal.
"Yeah, I had breakfast at Sonny's," he answered.
"Okay then, everything is packed and ready to go."
"Let's go. Everybody grab something and bring it to the car."

He opened the trunk and put what he could in it. He and Yolanda had to tie the rest of the stuff on the roof of the car in order to pack everything. They all piled in and were on their way to Inkster.

By the time he got back to Detroit it was eleven-thirty. He had just enough time to take a shower and freshen up a bit before he met Cathy at the library.

It was 12:14 when Jamal arrived at the library. He found a parking space and sat on the steps as he waited for Cathy. At least now he didn't have to worry about her blowing that damn horn as she normally did, he thought to himself. She was all right in his estimate—a little naive, he thought, but she had a good heart and good intentions; she showed an interest in humanity. Why couldn't all white people be like that?

He wondered what her mother was like, being that her family was somewhat wealthy. Probably snobbish, he reckoned, thinking they were better than most people—especially black people. Even if she found out he was black and she was helping him, she wouldn't object as it probably helped clear her conscience of assisting in the exploitation of the poor, which was no doubt how they obtained their wealth, he figured. He really didn't want to meet her and hoped Cathy never brought up the idea. Right in the middle of his thoughts he spotted the white Cougar with the black vinyl top and immediately knew it was her.

She found a parking space across the street. She looked lovely as she stepped out of the car waiting to cross the street. He stood up as she approached the library steps.

"Am I on time?" she asked, coming up the stairs.
"Actually you're a few minutes early this time."

They went into the library together and grabbed a table as they planned to be there a while.

"Well here we are professor. What is my first assignment?" she asked him.

"The first assignment in the world of self-education is to remove the illusion that two-thirds of the people, at least in this country, live under."

"Such as?" she asked.

"Such as the illusion of democracy, and you can only do that by examining the political system we live under using a dialectical approach."

"I don't quite understand," she said.

"Well the electoral collegiate system of voting as applied under the title of democracy is contradictory within itself, using the two-party system where the people never get a chance to elect the candidates. They are superimposed upon us by the two parties; the masses of the people usually don't favor either one but are forced to pick between the two. That, my lovely lady, ain't no democracy. The American dream is the biggest illusion cast upon the American people. Those that chase the dream without the means to make it come true wind up in prison or mental hospitals, become drug addicts or alcoholics, or end up losing the little they had trying to make it come true."

"Is that what happened to you?" she asked.

"Certainly, and the prison experience is what shocked me into reality."

"How was that?" she asked.

"While serving time in prison today, the majority of people you see are of African decent; it kinda makes you wonder, knowing that we are such a small percent of the nation's population. All you see getting transported back and forth to the courtrooms, to the jails, and off to prison, always in chains, are people of color, mostly blacks; you couldn't paint a better picture describing slavery. After seeing all this is when I realized that the American dream for us is a nightmare."

She was quite captivated by his analysis of situations regarding the system we lived under and his ability to articulate it. Would she have to go to prison to become such an analyst? she wondered. How did he develop such a keen insight into things? Why, with all the education that she had, was she not able to sort out these types of situations like he was able to? She was beginning to realize that there was something wrong with the educational system she was educated under; they were either hiding something or deceiving the people they were educating.

"So after I remove the illusion, then what do I do?"

"It has to be replaced with harsh reality, something most people don't want to face up to. For example, in prison, most people serving long sentences which will keep them in prison the rest of their lives all live with the illusion that one day soon their convictions will be overturned by the higher courts and they soon will be going home. When in reality only two or three cases out of a thousand may get overturned in a span of five years, while the rest sit and rot, you feel me—I mean, you get my point?"

"Oh yes, quite clear," she said and added, "What are some of the realities that I must face?"

"Well one of the biggest realities that you must face is that you don't have the freedom that you think you have in this country."

"Such as?" she said.

"Such as the so-called freedom guaranteed you by the Constitution. For instance, your First Amendment rights, freedom of speech, are a farce; men have been silenced for speaking out through such methods as assassination, imprisonment, exile, and straight out being barred from national broadcasting. Freedom to assemble—a joke; students were murdered on campus for protesting. A right to bear arms; humph! They changed that law in California as soon as black people started to assert that right—notably, the Black Panthers. Oh certainly, they'll tell you you have those rights, and you may have, as long as you don't try to assert them in a manner which isn't approved of by the controllers," he answered very definitely.

"Are there any more that you can think of?" she asked.

"There are plenty, but there is one in particular, and that is *justice*. If you're looking for any justice, it depends on who you are and what the circumstances are. For instance, for African-Americans there is none; for whites it depends on the circumstances."

"Can you give me a set of circumstances where I wouldn't receive justice?" she asked with anticipation.

"Certainly, put yourself in the same set of circumstances as Monica Lewinsky. Any time you're up against the rich and the powerful, justice flies out the window. I don't care who you are; if you're not in that circle, you don't stand a chance, be it in the courtroom, in front of those Senate committees, or anything connected to the power structure. To them, there is but one meaning, one interpretation of the word 'justice,' and that is 'just us.'"

"Gee, you're something else, " she said.

"Let's go to the bookshelf and see what we can find," he told her.

They strolled over to the section under philosophy, and he referred her to certain authors such as Camus, Jean Paul Sartre, Nietische, Marx, Plato, Tolstoy, and a few other heavyweights. Though she had heard some of the name, she never read any of their works. Jamal figured since he had her interest he would start her off with that type of literature to help raise her level of awareness, as she could be a great asset to the struggle. She picked out a couple of books and they went back to the table.

His mind had been taken off the situation in the hood as he became too relaxed in this type of environment. He began to ponder, *Why did I have to get tied up in this nonsense in the street?* It was the very thing he was trying to avoid. What he was doing at the moment was what he was really about, but he still felt obligated to help his nephew. Cathy could read his thoughts.

"You're thinking again," she said.

"Oh excuse me, I may have drifted off a minute."

"That's all right, I understand; your mind is on your nephew's situation."

"Yeah, this may be a big night tonight."

"Why is that?" she asked.

"Friday and Saturday nights are traditionally violent nights in the ghetto. They even named a pistol called the Saturday Night Special behind that tradition."

"Is there any particular reason why that happens?" she asked.

"In every major city highly populated by blacks, there are guaranteed homicides on weekend nights mainly due to the frustration of ghetto life, of never having enough of anything in the midst of the enormous wealth that surrounds them, the constant day-to-day struggle for survival, the feeling of being trapped, boxed in a cage of poverty. All this frustration comes out at the end of the week and is carried out against one another, as one always strikes out against that which is closest to them, which is one of the main purposes for segregation. Weekend nights are when most people congregate for some form of entertainment, and you can best believe when that many frustrated people are out together at one time, an eruption of violence is inevitable," he explained.

"So you are predicting an event happening tonight, directly associated with your nephew's gang?"

"First of all, they're not a gang. This is not gang war; this is about money, territory, control, and revenge. These are crews that came together for the purpose of making a little extra money, and their protection from other crews are each other. Second, to answer your question, these are the nights that a person is most likely to catch someone they're looking for, as everybody comes out on these nights to gather socially, except those who have extreme situations that causes them to lay low rather than run the risk of being killed or captured."

"Well, if this is so well known and predictable, why aren't the police roaming these areas to prevent this from happening?" she asked curiously.

Boy, she really is green, he thought to himself.

"You're forgetting something."

"What's that?" she asked.

"Were talking about the black community; the police don't even come right away when they're called. And by the time they do show up, the victims are dead or wounded and the perpetrators are on the other side of town. Life is cheap in the black community, as demonstrated by the police department and D.A.s office's lack of interest in solving crimes committed against people of African-American descent."

"So that is why your nephew's friends are taking matters in their own hands?"

"Well not really, because in street life there is such a thing called street justice; in other words, people on the street don't look to the law to handle their problems. In the street you handle your own problems; Only the everyday nine-to-five square John people rely on the police. To street people the police are the enemy."

Cathy was quite amazed at how different her lifestyle was from the street people. She had learned that they definitely didn't consider themselves part of society. They were not bad people, they just rejected this society and lived by their own code. She began to understand why many of them dropped out of school, didn't seek employment, didn't go to church, didn't vote, didn't register for the draft, and basically didn't give a hoot about being accepted. They were totally the opposite from the blacks she had gone to college with, who wanted to be socially accepted by mainstream America, who would fight and die for this country, who believed in and relied on this system and strove to become a part of it.

It was nearly three-thirty when Cathy looked at her watch.

"Oh wow! How time flies. You want to go grab something to eat?" she asked.

"Yeah, we can do that. Matter of fact, since we're already downtown we can go to Greektown again."

"That's fine with me," she said.

She left in her car and he in Yolanda's. She was surprised he had driven; as long as he had spent in prison she didn't think he could drive at all. They went to Tony's and had dinner before they ended up going their separate ways; Cathy back to a quiet, safe little place in the suburbs and Jamal back to a drug-infested, bullets-flying ghetto.

Chapter 14

"Yo Raymond! You know your name come up as the one they want to, take care of that business over at Steve's Restaurant," B-light, who was Bunchy's first lieutenant, told him.

"You talking about Lonzo, right?" Raymond asked.

"Yeah, he's next on the agenda.

"They want me to just walk up into the restaurant and get him?" Raymond stated more so than asked.

"Man, whatever it takes, but you gotta get yo man—tonight said," B-light emphasized.

"I ain't got no problem with that, but I ain't trying to be seen either."

"Lay on him in the parking lot, that's how I'd get him," B-light said.

"Yeah, but look, who I got to use to drive the car?" he told B-light.

"Let me see if I can get Ponce to drive; he ain't gon' punk-out on you."

Raymond didn't mind taking care of the hit, he just wanted to make sure he got away with it. This was not like the regular little beefs in the hood; these were murder assignments. He had shot people before, but he was no killer. These kinds of assignments were for people like Byrd, Li'l All, and Blood Lawson. The idea of having one of them take care of it and he would pay them crossed his mind, but he hadn't had enough time to make that arrangement.

Jamal drove back to the motel from the library. It was almost five-thirty, so he had enough time to check by the house on twenty-third, then call Yolanda to see how things were coming along out in Inkster at his mama's house.

When he got home everything was just the way he left it. The first thing he checked for was the guns and explosives; they were still there and he felt relieved.

He called his mother's house and Yolanda answered the phone. His mother was not at home as usual; she was a very outgoing woman who attended a lot of social gatherings. That was good for Yolanda, as she would have more control over things while their mother was attending her gatherings. She mentioned that outside of the kids acting up a bit, everything else seemed to be going all right. He told her that nothing else had occurred in the developing drug war to his knowledge, at least not as of yet. She herself was relieved to hear that.

After he finished his conversation with Yolanda, he put the T.V. on to catch the news. A young man in the neighborhood was found dead that morning in his garage, shot to death four times in what seemed to be a drug-related incident. Jamal didn't recognize the name, but it happened on Bangor Street, just a few streets over from where he lived.

"It must have been one of Y.K.2. Fifty Grand's people as this is their hood," he thought out loud. He had to find out for certain, for if so, things were ready to escalate. He would find out tonight from Li'l Al, who would know everything he'd need to know regarding the developing war.

Damn, there's no way around this now, he thought; he'd have to bring in Byrd and Blood for sure. Li'l Al's crew would be neutral in this war. They could be a great asset to him, and he would find out tonight. He went to his room and pulled out his foot locker that he had shipped to himself from prison. He took out all of his belongings and put them on the bed. He pulled up a chair and slid the trap door back that led to the attic and grabbed the duffle bag that contained the weapons and the other which contained the explosives and put them in the foot locker, then threw a few clothes on top of them and locked it. He had made up his mind to take them to the motel with him when it got dark, and even if the maid cleaned up in the morning, she couldn't get inside the foot locker. Right then the phone rang, and he picked up the receiver.

"Hello! Is this Jamal?"

"Yeah, who is this?"

"It's Raymond, yo! I got the Glock, but you have to go over to Charley's to pick it up. just ask for Short Dog; he already knows you're coming."

"What's up, anything new?" Jamal asked.

"Yeah, but I can't talk now. I'll holler at you when I get a chance."

"Yeah, all right, you know the two places where I'll be at, right?"

"Yeah I know," Raymond said.

"All right, check you later," Jamal sad, wondering what it was Raymond had to tell him as he hung up the phone.

He could tell something was up by the way Raymond was acting—a little jittery and overly cautious. He knew he couldn't ask where he was. The way things were going you could say very little over the phone. Jamal didn't like waiting around for something he wanted and he wanted the Glock bad, so he immediately drove over to Charley's. Charley's was like a motorcycle club where a lot of people hung out. It was converted into a club-house from a garage on an open lot that was used to work on cars; now it was full of Hondas and Yamahas.

It was also a place used to fence stolen goods; however, there were no drugs sold there so as to keep the place from being raided by the police and risk being closed down. When Jamal arrived he saw all sorts of people hanging out, drinking forty ounces of beer; some were working on their cycles, souping them up for racing, which was a big event in Detroit. Loud music boomed from the speakers in the clubhouse, females were roaming around in their tight shorts, and some people were dancing outside of the clubhouse; people were barbecuing out in the field. It looked like a big cookout or picnic. The first person he saw was a big light-skinned dude with a ponytail sucking on a barbecue rib.

"Yo! My man, you know Short Dog?"

"Yeah, everybody know Short Dog."

"Where can I find him?" Jamal asked.

"Go to the back room of the clubhouse; you'll find him."

As soon as he walked into the clubhouse he noticed it was set up like a union hall—chairs lined up in a row in front of a platform.

There was a door on both sides of the platform to what he assumed to be the back room. There were a few people sitting around in a discussion not really paying him any attention as he walked in, so he went to the door on the right-hand side and knocked on it. A big fellow about six-feet-five inches tall came to the door.

"I'm looking for Short-Dog," Jamal said and then added, "he should be expecting me; my name is Jamal."

The big fellow stepped out in the hallway and motioned for Jamal to raise his hands to be frisked. Jamal hesitantly raised his hands

"Don't take this personal, just a customary practice," the big fellow stated then motioned for Jamal to enter ahead of him. They entered one door which led to another one. As Jamal entered the next door he saw four men sitting at a table playing poker. The big man hollered out.

"Yo Short! Somebody here to see ya."

Short Dog got up from the table. He was about the size of Li'l Al, but he was younger and didn't have that ferocious look Li'l Al did.

"Jamal, right?" Short Dog asked.

"Yeah, Raymond's uncle."

"Yeah, I know. You probably don't remember me; I was just a shorty when you went up state for shooting that cop, but hold tight. I got that for ya." He went into a little office that set off to the left and came out with a shopping bag and handed it to Jamal.

"All gift-wrapped for ya, dog.

"My man, I appreciate that, brother."

"No sweat, glad to see ya out, take care."

"You too," Jamal said as he stepped off.

On his way home Jamal was thinking how easily available such weapons of this caliber were to get a hold of and the youth were the ones who had access to them. *Too much of a coincidence,* he thought. After all, they were being used against each other.

He was glad that Short Dog had used a shopping bag to put the Glock in. That way nothing would look suspicious to the neighbors; it looked as if he had just come from shopping.

The minute he got home he went directly to his room to check if the foot locker was still there and opened it for inspection; everything was just as he had left it. He took out the gift-wrapped package from the shopping bag and began to unwrap it. "Man they really wrapped this thing," he said to himself. When he finally got it opened it was brand new, and there was another small package with the bullets in there. It began to register upon him that Raymond was making it adequately convenient for him to make his move when the time was right.

It would be getting dark soon, so he fixed himself something small to eat and turned the T.V. on to the news. Nothing new had happened since the last time he had listened to it, so he cut it off and looked out the window. It was already dark so he went into his room, put the Glock and bullets in the foot locker, and carried it on his shoulder out the door and to the car. He thought it best to put it in the trunk.

He locked the house and drove carefully to the motel. When he arrived in the parking lot of the motel he scanned the area to see if anyone was out and about. Satisfied, he carried the foot locker up the stairs to his room. In case anyone did see him, they would think he was on some type of vacation trip. He put the locker in the closet, then checked his watch; it was 8:20. Byrd and Li'l Al would be pulling up at any moment if nothing had come up. He began reading the paper when he heard a knock at the door.

"Who is it?"

"Byrd and Li'l Al."

He opened the door. "Man y'all right on time," Jamal told them. "Have a seat."

"Yeah, it's about to get ugly out there," Li'l As said in a rugged tone of voice.

"That's what I need to know; give it to me straight."

Li'l Al sat on the opposite end of the bed. Byrd, on the other end, pulled out a pint of Crown Royal and three cups. After everybody poured their drink Li'l Al spoke. "Here's the latest. One of Y.K.2.'s boys got slumped over on Bangor Street late last night, I guess they found his body this morning. Now, Y.K.2. is definitely ready to retaliate tonight. Once that goes down, it's open warfare, cut and dry."

"Okay, since it's beyond negotiating a truce, I want to hit as close to the top man as possible and strike hard where it will carry such an impact that they'll want to talk. I got some heavy-duty stuff that they ain't use to seeing, and believe me, after they get hit with this they're going to be trying to get out of town."

"Oh yeah, you holding like that?" Al said.

"Yeah, I got some high-powered explosives. I'm trying to blow these fools off the map in round one so it won't be no round two, you feel me?"

"Yeah, I feel ya," Li'l Al answered.

"So what's the plan?" Byrd asked with anticipation.

"All right, I'll handle the explosives," Jamal said. "I'll need you and Blood to cut down any clown that comes out of that spot. I'll need you and your crew, Li'l Al, to hold us down in case of any interference."

"So who we going after?" Byrd asked Li'l Al.

"It's gotta be Crusher, Butch Dog, or Sid; that's their power. You take down any one of them, you'll take a big hunk out of the Down River Mob, you see what I'm saying? They're the ones that are holding the front down," Li'l Al said with passion.

He knew all the ins and outs to everything that went on in the drug world, for that was his livelihood, that's who he survived off of.

"The way I see it, either they're going to fold after that or they're coming strong with all they got. Either way don't make no difference to me,," Byrd said, stating his position.

"Have you hollered at Blood?" Jamal asked Byrd.

"Yeah, he said whenever you're ready, just give him a holla. You know Blood don't like to come out until the action starts."

"All right Byrd, you lay low tonight. Me and Li'l Al is going over and check out that spot. Let Blood know that we're rollin' tomorrow. I'll beep you and let you know what time we'll meet up here.

"Gotcha," Byrd said and added, "I see you got you a ride, huh?"

"Yeah, I took Yolanda and the kids out to my mom's house and kept the ride."

Aight, I'm gon' bounce." Byrd looked out the window to check the parking lot, then creped on out the door.

"So how you think the Down River Mob is going to react after they take a hit tonight?" Jamal asked Li'l Al.

"The same way they did when it first jumped off with Fifty Grand; they'll try to make a big impact."

"So you're saying another possible massacre?"

"Yeah, if they can pull it off."

"But they need somebody from the inside to pull off something like that."

"Exactly, and it can happen if they can get to the right person; I don't know how the Y.K.2. boys are laying on that tip, but I'd be willing to bet that there's a weak link somewhere within them."

"Yeah, no doubt," Jamal said, almost in a whisper.

They finished their drinks with some small talk when Li'l Al jumped up and said, "You ready to go case that out?"

"Yeah, let's roll," Jamal quickly reacted and they quietly left out of the door.

Chapter 15

Raymond was a little nervous as they pulled into the parking lot of Steve's Restaurant.

"Pull up alongside of that truck so the car can be blocked out of view," Raymond told Ponce.

"You want me to back in, right?"

"Yeah, we gotta have a quick getaway."

Ponce backed the car in just enough to keep the entrance of the restaurant in view in order to catch who went in and who went out.

"Can you see inside the joint from here?" Raymond asked.

"Not clearly," Ponce replied, appearing calm.

"Check it, you need to go up by the door and see if you can spot our vic. You can't miss him; he's sporting a white baseball cap turned backwards."

"I can't just go up there peeping in; it's gon' look too suspicious, me just standing around."

"Don't just stand around. Ask somebody for some directions or something."

"Yeah, aight."

Ponce casually got out of the car and walked up by the door to the restaurant. He took his time until he saw a young lady come out with her food order.

"Excuse me, miss, is this the only restaurant around here?"

"No, there's another one about three blocks down the Street."

As she explained the direction, Ponce peeped through the plate glass window and spotted the white baseball cap. He thanked the young lady and strolled back to the car.

"Did you see him?" Raymond asked reluctantly, in hopes that the vic didn't show up, as that would let him off the hook, at least for now.

"Yeah, I spotted him. He's in there kicking it with a couple of his boys. The joint is crowded, too."

"Well I guess we'll have to wait 'til he makes a move," Raymond said, more so speaking to himself.

They just sat and chilled in anticipation. Ponce had the radio turned up loud, bobbing his head and patting the steering wheel to the music.

"Man, cut that music down. I can't concentrate."

"Damn, you buggin' like that?" Ponce jagged at him.

Raymond was concentrating on how he could get his man and cut down on his chances of being seen, when suddenly he spotted his vic.

"Yo! Start the car and keep it running; this fool is about to come out. I can see the white baseball cap near the door."

Raymond cracked the door open and quietly slid one foot out of the car as he timed his vic. As soon as the white cap started moving he started moving. Lonzo, Raymond's vic, was with two other dudes and Raymond didn't know if they were Down River Boys or not. It really didn't matter. If they got hit they just got hit; that's the way it goes, Raymond rationalized.

He carried the Glock he had between a folded newspaper to conceal it; he had gotten that idea from a T.V. program. By the time Lonzo reached his car, Raymond opened fire about ten feet away from him. People immediately started scattering as Lonzo fell up against the car. One of the dudes that was with him reached inside his waist band and Raymond kept firing, hitting him also. The other fellow with him ducked around the car out of the way. Ponce pulled the car out in the aisle, waiting for Raymond.

"Let's go man!" Ponce hollered.

Raymond backed away and ran and jumped in the car as Ponce was taking off. Ponce hit the driveway to the main street and took off into traffic, there was so much commotion it was hard to say if anyone had spotted them. They made it back to Charley's safe and sound and checked in with B-light.

"How we looking, dog?" B-light more or less asked either one of them.

"Everthing's straight; that been taken care of," Raymond said with pride. He felt good in one sense, as he had finally earned his stripes; however, on the other hand, he also knew that if he had been seen he would be targeted by the Down River Boys as their next victim.

Jamal dropped off Li'l Al after they finished casing the spot where Crusher, from the Down River Mob, distributed the drugs to each group of the mob. He was glad they didn't have to try to get inside, as it would have been virtually impossible without inside help. The way he planned it, he would smoke them out first; if they weren't already blown to smithereens, then he would have Byrd and Blood chop them down. It was about 11:00 P.M., so he decided to stop by Steve's Restaurant to get something to eat since it stayed open all night and had the best food in town. As he turned on to Grand River, he could see red lights flashing coming from the direction of Steve's. As he moved closer, he could see the crowd of people and police cars. It was evident that something big had happened. His instincts told him that this was connected to the developing drug war.

He couldn't help but think of his nephew, but there were too many police in the area for him to hang around, as he was strapped. So he decided to go to Burger King instead. He pulled into the nearest Burger King drive-through and ordered fish and fries, then drove back to the motel as quick as possible, without drawing any attention, as it was a bad time to be on the streets, especially riding with a pistol. As soon as he got to his room he turned on the T.V. to the local news to catch the nights events. Then it came; BREAKING NEWS: *SHOOTING AT STEVE'S RESTAURANT*—three people shot, two dead, one wounded.

"No one apprehended in what police believe is an ongoing drug war related to the Vinewood massacre."

The bodies of the two who were killed were not identified as of yet. There was no way of knowing who struck who. He wouldn't be able to find out until the next day, there was too much heat for either Byrd or Li'l Al to travel tonight. He banked on what Li'l Al had told him earlier about Y.K.2. boys striking tonight; however, that left them vulnerable. He would definitely have to strike tomorrow to try to put a cap on this thing before something happened to his nephew.

There was nothing else he could do tonight; he definitely had a big day coming up tomorrow.

Chapter 16

As Yolanda began to get the kids ready for church, she couldn't help but think of Raymond, her first child, her oldest son, the only one she really had to worry about at the present. She had heard the news about the boy being found dead a few streets over from where they lived and also about last night's shooting at Steve's Restaurant. Raymond was more than likely involved in some way; she could feel it, a woman's intuition. Why hadn't Jamal called? He was her only source of information regarding Raymond's situation. Now she had to worry about whether he had gotten involved. She knew him well; he would come to Raymond's rescue no matter what, even if he didn't approve of Raymond's activities. She had another brother and two older sisters who lived in California. One had married and recently moved to Colorado.

Jamal was the youngest and the only one in the family who had been in trouble: the so-called black sheep.

She called the house twice the day before and yesterday but got no answer. She figured Jamal was probably staying at the motel and Raymond was with the crew he belonged to. As she began to fix breakfast, the phone rang. Red picked up the phone. "Mama! Jamal on the phone."

Yolanda raced to the phone. "Hello! It's about time."

"I've been busy; there's been a lot going on in the last day or so."

"Have you talked with Raymond?" she asked.

"Yeah, I talked with him yesterday."

"Does he appear to be in any trouble?"

"It's hard to tell," he lied. He didn't want to worry her more than she was already worring.

"Nobody's staying in the house I assume?"

"Not right now. I'm staying at the motel, and there's no telling where Raymond is staying."

"I've been listening to the news, and it appears that there's a war going on over there," she said.

"Yeah, it don't look good right now; it's open season. That's why I got you and the kids up outta there."

"Well, as soon as you find out something about that fool boy of mine, let me know."

"Awright, take it easy."

"Yeah, you too; bye now."

Jamal bought a newspaper on his way into Sonny's Restaurant and ordered breakfast. The shootings from last night made front-page news; police were seeking a young male in his late teens as the assailant and an unknown getaway driver. They gave no other description of the assailant. He thought for a second. *Could it have been Raymond?* then quickly removed the thought from his mind. Hell, that could have been any of a thousand youths in the city, he supposed.

The one thing he didn't want to do was to jump to conclusions. He would have to wait until he got confirmed accounts of what happened—as to what crew got hit, what crew did the hit, and if it was for sure that this was a connected incidence. The only one he knew of who could confirm all of that was Li'l Al. He was stuck until he had a chance to talk to him. He finished his meal and went back to the motel.

"Yo Raymond, you gonna have to lay low. I think somebody might have recognized you in the parking lot," B-light told him.

"How you know that?" Raymond asked.

"Somebody told me they heard your name being kicked around about what happened last night."

"Damn, somebody always running off at the mouth," Raymond said.

"Yeah, you know how that goes."

"I got to get in touch with my uncle, man."

"You know where he's at?"

"Yeah, but I can't risk going over there."

"What you want me to do, go over there for you?"

"Naw, get in touch with Goochi and tell him to tell Li'l Al I need to see him, it's important."

Raymond did not want to expose where his uncle took residence, except to those who were personal friends of his. B-light left the hideout and made it over to Charley's to deliver the message to Goochi. Goochi was one of Li'l Al's crew and immediately contacted Li'l Al.

Chapter 17

Jamal was listening to the news when he heard a knock at the door.

"Who is it?"

"Li'l Al."

"Damn, this must be important," Jamal said as he let Li'l Al in.

"You got that right," Li'l Al said in a serious voice.

"What's up?"

"I got a message from your nephew. I guess he didn't trust nobody else; anyway, he wants you to know that they got him fingered as the trigger-man at Steve's."

"Who, the police?" Jamal asked curiously.

"Naw, that's just the word on the street."

"God man! They turned that boy into a killer. I'm really gonna have to step this thing up now; they gonna be coming for his ass," Jamal said as the killer instinct rose in him.

"So what you want to do, set this up for tonight?" Li'l Al asked with anticipation.

"Yeah, I got to."

"What time you want me to round my crew up?"

"Have them ready by ten o'clock. We'll meet up at Charley's. I'll have Byrd and Blood come by about nine."

"That's a bet," Li'l Al said, moving toward the door.

Jamal looked at his watch; it was about two-thirty. He had to sit back a minute and collect his thoughts. This had gotten way more serious than he had anticipated. He never would have figured Raymond to be chosen for the trigger-man; it didn't fit his character. All Raymond wanted to do was make a few extra dollars; he never wanted to hurt anyone if he didn't have to. This had to be imposed upon him as an obligation to his crew. How could he tell Yolanda, even though she halfway expected something like this to happen as long as he was in the game. That's just the way the game was played out on the streets. He also needed to get in touch with Cathy to let her know he might have to let the job go. He went to the phone booth and called Cathy; he was lucky she was there.

"Hello, who's speaking?"

"Jamal."

"Oh! How are you? What a surprise."

"I'm all right; are you busy?"

"No, not at all."

"Can we meet at the library?"

"When, right now?" Cathy questioned, somewhat alarmed.

"Can you make it by three?"

"Sure, I'll be there."

"Good enough, I'll see you there," Jamal said as he hung up the phone.

He beeped Byrd while he was there. He waited for the connection. The phone rang, and he picked up the receiver. "Yo Byrd."

"Yeah, what's up?"

"This is Jamal."

"Oh go 'head," Byrd said.

"Can you swoop up Blood and meet me at the room at nine o'clock?"

"Yeah man, we'll be there," Byrd agreed with eagerness.

Jamal hung up the phone, went to the car, and decided to go straight to the library to wait for Cathy. After he found a parking space, he went to his favorite spot on the library steps and began to read his book as he waited. He was there about three minutes when he spotted the white Cougar. She found a parking space a couple of buildings down and then came swinging up the steps.

The urgency of the matter told her something had come up, as he had never contacted her on a moment's notice like this. When she reached him she blurted out, "At your command, sir."

"Let's go inside," he said sternly.

They went in and grabbed a table in the corner.

"Are you all right?" she asked.

"Oh yeah, I'm all right, but things are a little hazy right now."

"A little hazy, what's that mean?' She was puzzled.

"What I'm trying to get at is, the way things are going I don't know if I'll be able to show up for work in the morning."

"Oh Jamal, I hope you're not mixed up in anything."

"No, I'm not mixed up in anything, but I'll have to keep a close eye out for my nephew. Things are heating up."

"Well if you can't show up for work in the morning at least give them a legitimate excuse."

Damn, she's not getting the point, he said to himself.

"That'll be hard to do because I can't guarantee if I'll be able to show up the next morning after that or any more mornings period. I'll have to play everything by ear."

"Gee, I'm sorry to hear that because it may be a blue moon before you can find another job," she said, somewhat irritated by his coldness.

"That's the way the ball bounces. I just wanted to let you know so you won't feel betrayed."

"Oh, don't think I don't understand your position. I just hate that you were forced into it like this."

"I've grown rather used to it; in other words, I've learned to except the unexpected."

"Is there any way that I can help?" she asked sincerely.

"Not at the moment, you've been a great help already, and I'm truly grateful for your sincere efforts."

"I just wish things were normal, where we could get together and study. I've learned so much in so little time spent with you."

"Well perhaps when this blows over things will return back to normal," he said with a ray of hope.

"Have you eaten yet?" she asked.

"Naw, would you like to go to Greektown?"

"Oh I'd love to."

They left and rode in Cathy's car to Tony's. There were just a few people in Tony's, which made Jamal feel more comfortable. The waitress was used to seeing them together now and no one else paid them any particular attention.

"Do you really think something may happen to your nephew?" she asked him.

"It's hard to say; when you live the street life you live from day to day, never really knowing what tomorrow will bring. Risks are always high. You live by the gun, you die by the gun—a common acceptance. This sort of life is imposed upon most of us from birth in the ghetto; the few that escape usually turn out to be sell-outs. When you live that lifestyle you never sit back and plan a career. Most of our futures are cut short by prison, drugs, alcohol, or a bullet. We live with that reality, and my nephew is no exception. All I'm trying to do is buy him some time," Jamal stated flatly.

Cathy was stunned by such a harsh reality. She understood that you had to be a strong person to live with that type of reality. She wished there was something she could do to help fix things, but deep in her heart she knew there was nothing she could do.

"Aren't there other avenues open, such as music, sports, the film industry?"

"Why certainly, which will only accommodate a small percentage of our people—something like one and a half percent—while the rest perish in that dilemma."

"Well, can't that be fixed or changed?"

"My people are afraid of change. We have become so used to this wretched condition it has become an accepted way of life. We have been convinced by living under these conditions for so long that it was meant for us to struggle to survive. To change means to upset the order of things and confront the system head on, which will ultimately call for sacrifice, something, I hate to say, my people are not willing to do as of yet."

"Well, I just want you to know that you can call on me for anything within my reach," Cathy offered.

"That's good to know," Jamal said as he drifted off into thought.

They finished their meal mostly in silence, and Cathy took him back to the library to pick up his car. Jamal drove back to the motel, and Cathy drove back to the suburbs.

Chapter 18

It was around 8:00 P.M., and Blood would be showing up in a little while. Jamal would go over the plans with them and then head on out to Charley's to meet up with Li'l Al and his crew. He poured himself a small drink of the rum that was left so as to calm the excitement of the drama that had arisen inside of him in anticipation of the forthcoming events that ached at him—not so much as to what he was about to do but what it was over and who it was with. He was ever conscious that these were not his real enemies, but he rationalized it with the fact that they were a problem within the black community, but then again so was his nephew, which seemed to eat at him even more. However, he sincerely felt that this move may put a cap on this whole thing.

He turned on the T.V. to the evening news to see if anything else had happened. Nothing new had occurred since last night's shooting at Steve's. Then something came across the screen: **NEW LEADS IN THE VINEWOOD MASSACRE**. But the police department did not want to divulge any information as of yet. Jamal figured that they were either bluffing to make it appear that they were about to solve the case, in order to calm the community, or they were about to grab a scapegoat.

He got up to change the channel when he heard a knock at the door.

"Who is it?"

"Byrd and Blood."

As he opened the door he noticed the golf bag that Blood was carrying and the twinkle in Byrd's eyes. He greeted them both with hugs and hefty handshakes, an indication of his appreciation for their assistance, a gesture of true comradeship. When they entered, Jamal invited them to sit on the bed. Blood was looking mean as ever and Byrd, as usual, a little paranoid but not as much as when he had first started coming to the motel room.

"So what time do we roll?" Blood asked.

"In about forty-five minutes, but first I want to go over a few things." He went to the closet to get the foot locker out. Byrd leaned over to see what he was doing. After he dragged the foot locker out Byrd seemed somewhat relieved. As Jamal pulled everything out, you could see Blood's eyes light up with excitement.

"You got some high-powered stuff there," Blood said.

"This is what's going to smoke them out of the house."

"Yeah, that's if they make it out," Byrd said.

"No doubt it's powerful enough to shake the whole joint up, but some of them'll have enough time to come up out of there. That's where you and Blood come in."

He began to go over the plan with them when he saw a light flash outside the window and said, "Yo! Feds!"

Byrd jumped up immediately and looked out the window. He saw the cop looking at the van he had parked in the parking lot and whispered, "Yo Blood, they checking the van out."

Blood popped open the golf bag and pulled out an assault rifle and a sawed-off pump shotgun. He tossed the shotgun to Byrd. Byrd saw the two policemen coming toward the motel and assumed they were coming for him or Blood or maybe both of them. Someone had put them on their trail, he figured. There were three all together; two of them had gotten out of an unmarked car and a uniformed cop stayed in his squad car, Byrd coldly calculated his move.

"Yo Blood, I'll catch them coming up the steps and you get the joker in the squad car."

Byrd and Blood knew they were trapped; there was no other exit out of there. This was the moment they had long anticipated. Byrd went out of the door with the pump in his hand. Jamal picked up the Glock and the TEC 9 and followed Byrd. *Boom! Boom!* You could hear the loud blast from the pump, and from the street you could see the burst of gunfire. Byrd dropped both of them; they never stood a chance.

A white female who was talking to the officers in the squad car heard the blast when it went off. She was horrified as she saw the two plainclothes detectives fall to the ground. The officer in the squad car reached for his radio when a shot rang out from the motel window and hit him dead in the forehead. He lay slumped over the steering wheel. Byrd and Jamal were hurrying toward the van with Blood bringing up the rear, a duffle bag in one hand and a golf bag in the other. As they approached the van the female who had been talking with the officers stood there in awe. As she met Byrd's gaze, she knew it was over.

Boom! Another blast from the pump rang out as Byrd never hesitated. The female fell to the ground. They all jumped into the van and Byrd sped off. He went a couple of exits down and hit the freeway. They rode the freeway until Byrd came up on the ramp that would take them to Blood's neighborhood. Blood told Byrd to pull up to the alley where they would ditch the van and then cut through a pathway that would take them two streets over and they would hop into another ride and make it to Byrd's hideout on the Eastside. They made it to the car and sped off. Once they hit the freeway they would be pretty much in the clear, as no one saw them get into that car. The police would be looking for the van.

The news of the incident came across the T.V., the radio, and traveled fast in the streets: **POLICE GUNNED DOWN IN COLD BLOOD IN THE PARKING LOT OF THE CADILLAC MOTEL.**

When Li'l Al heard the news he knew it had to be Jamal, Byrd, and Blood. The police had come up on them at the wrong time, he figured. They were all hardcore street dudes who had done long prison terms, who killed out of survival on the streets, and would not be taken back to prison if they could help it. Li'l Al himself was of the same caliber and would have done the same thing; he just hated that Jamal had gotten caught up in it, as he hadn't been out a good month yet.

Chapter 19

Yolanda, her mother, and the kids were all sitting in front of the T.V. waiting for the eleven o'clock news as an earlier bulletin had flashed across the screen. One of the kids was watching a program when it flashed across the screen about policemen being gunned down at the Cadillac Motel, which was close to their neighborhood in Detroit. But more important, it's where Jamal had rented a room. Yolanda was almost certain that her brother was involved, knowing that he had been with Byrd and also given the fact that he was expecting some guns from Raymond. In her estimate, it was just too much of a coincidence for it not to be them. She had figured all along that he was up to something, hanging around with characters like Byrd and Blood Lawson.

The moment had arrived: "**Special news bulletin**: A man is being sought in connection with tonight's murders of three policemen and a white female: Jamal Rush, African-American male, age thirty, ex-convict recently released from Michigan's Department of Corrections after serving thirteen years for armed robbery and attempted murder of a police office." A picture of him appeared on the screen with a caption: *Caution, do not try to arrest, call for backup, suspect is armed and extremely dangerous and is believed to be in the company of other armed individuals.*

"That's Jamal!" the kids blurted out.

"That boy has really done it now. He's got himself in a mess of trouble," the grandmother said.

"Mama, you don't know if he done anything. He's just a suspect because he had a room at the motel and his record," Yolanda defended.

"Well I wouldn't want to be in his shoes. That boy has always been hardheaded, just like his father, won't listen to nobody," her mother emphasized.

"Jamal gon' shoot 'em if they come after him," Pooch said.

"Boy! Shut up, I mean that," Yolanda hollered at him. The baby in the crib started crying.

"Now see what you caused."

"I ain't caused that."

"You going to cause me to whip your butt if you don't shut your mouth."

"Why don't you put them to bed. You know they have to get up in the morning," the grandmother told her.

"That's a good point; all right everybody, let's hit the sack, school in the morning."

"We want to see the news," Red pleaded.

"You already seen the news, now get that butt to bed. I'm not going to tell you again."

They all went to bed thinking about the incident.

"Yo Raymond, you seen the news about your uncle?" B-light asked him.

"Yeah, that's messed up. He ain't been home three weeks."

"Goddamn that dude go hard."

"We don't know if that's him that done it, though."

"Yeah, you right, but they think he done it because of his record."

"Yeah, I know. He's definitely cut like that, but I don't know if he done that."

"They might try to kill him on sight," B-light stated.

"Yeah, but that ain't going to be easy either 'cause he's already expecting that," Raymond defended.

"Yo, them Down River Boys are going to be kind of leery about taking you out behind what they think your uncle did because they're going to figure your uncle ain't got nothing to lose."

"Yeah, you might have a point."

"Yo! B-light," a voice from downstairs hollered up.

"What's up?" B-light hollered back.

"Raymond up there?" the voice said again.

"Who wants to know?"

"This Short Dog."

"Yeah, come on up."

Short Dog raced up the stairs. "Hey what's up Raymond. I got a message from your uncle."

"Oh yeah?" Raymond said with excitement.

"He wants you to get in touch with your mother and tell her the car is in the parking lot of the motel, if the police haven't impounded it, and that he's all right and don't know nothing about what happened at the motel."

"I'm gonna handle that, good looking out, Short Dog."

"Yeah any time, I sho hope he can come out from under all that."

"Yeah me too. It's gonna be kind of rough, though."

"I'll holla back," Short Dog said as he raced back down the steps.

Everyone at the school where Jamal worked was talking about the incident. Jamal had become a ghetto celebrity overnight, a hero in his hood, for that which he was being accused of was considered a heroic act on the streets, especially in a city like Detroit where police brutality was a common occurrence, which made the police an enemy to the people. Anyone who had the courage to stand up against them received the highest of honors on the street level.

"Catrina, I can't believe we hired someone like that to work here," Mr. Johnson said to her.

"He didn't seem to be a bad fellow," Catrina shot back.

"They never do. They are the worst kind, the ones who have the ability to deceive you."

"I don't think he deceived anybody. He had good intentions, and we still don't know all the circumstances surrounding the incident."

"My God, Catrina, sounds as though you had a crush on him."

"Not really. I just got to know him a little better than most here did."

"Who recommended him anyway?"

"The recommendation came through Mr. Carrington, but I think it was his daughter who actually referred him."

"Sounds like something she would do, acting as one of those liberals," Mr. Johnson said in a disgusted voice.

"Well you can't fault her; she was doing what she thought to be a good deed."

"Mr. Carrington will have to answer to Grand Master of this school for this," Mr. Johnson predicted.

"Who, Mr. London?"

"That's right."

Champ was in the student's lounge talking to a few of the students about Jamal's fate.

"Yeah, that was my man; we was up the way together, and he had just got out too, trying to go straight. I don't know how he got caught up like that."

"Aw man, if they don't kill him they gonna give him forever and a day," one of the students said.

"Yeah, it don't make no difference whatever happens; he can handle it. He's a soldier. Don't get that twisted," Champ said arrogantly.

Cathy was at her girlfriend Jean's house drinking tea in the living room and chatting when the bulletin flashed across the screen. She was momentarily stunned.

Jean noticed the look on Cathy's face and asked, "Cathy, what's wrong? Are you all right? You look as though you've seen a ghost."

"I can't believe it," Cathy said.

"Can't believe what?"

"That's my friend, the one I've been telling you about."

"Oh my God, do you think he did all that?"

"I don't think so; he's far too intelligent to do something like that while he has a room at the same motel registered in his name."

"Well, why do you think he's the prime suspect?"

"Probably because of what he went to prison for. I think there was an officer shot in that incident."

"Oh I get it, they're making a connection," Jean said.

"Right, and his prison record is coming back to haunt him."

"Will you be able to help him?"

"How can I help him? I don't know where he is." Cathy said angrily, but she was more angry at the circumstances that wouldn't allow her to help the man she had grown fond of.

"Do you think he will turn himself in if he didn't do it?" Jean asked.

"I doubt it. He has very little faith in the justice system or any part of this system; as a matter of fact, he'll stay on the run until they either catch or kill him."

"It shouldn't have to be that way if he didn't do anything," Jean said.

"You're absolutely right, but that's the way it is for people of color in this country, especially African-Americans," Cathy stated, amazed at herself for answering in the same manner as Jamal would have without even thinking about it beforehand. She realized now that Jamal had had a powerful impact upon her way of thinking.

Later on that day when the news came on, they gave a more detailed account of what had happened. Witnesses had told police that they heard gunshots and saw the two officers fall to the ground, then heard another shot and saw a flash come from one of the motel windows when the officer in the squad car was hit. They also saw a white female talking to the officer in the squad car before he was shot. After the officer was struck down, two men came running from the motel into the parking lot; both had guns out and another shot rang out, hitting the female as the men approached the van that was in the parking lot. As the two men hopped in the van a third individual came running from the motel with what appeared to be a golf bag thrown over his shoulders; he hopped in the van and the van sped away. None of the men could be identified; all of the victims were fatally wounded.

"Wow! Did you hear that? A female was murdered also," Jean said.

"Well probably because she would have been able to identify the assailants."

"Detroit is a dangerous place to be caught in at night."

"I can't argue with you there," Cathy agreed.

Blood was pacing the floor in the basement of Byrd's hideout after watching the last account of the news.

"I thought you said didn't nobody see nothing," Blood questioned Byrd again.

"Naw, I said couldn't nobody identify nobody; it happened too fast and it was too dark."

"For real, it don't matter in my case, I'm dead meat anyway."

"We all dead meat. Suckers on the street talk too much, always speculating," Blood said, letting Jamal know that they'd all sink together.

"Yeah, speculate you right into the grave," Byrd agreed.

"We just got to lay low; Snake and Li'l Al is our contact out there."

"Damn, this shit happened at a bad time, but maybe it was meant to happen. This is where the real fight is at anyway."

"There you go with that revolutionary dream. Them fools out there don't care nothing about that; they too busy chasing a buck or some chick," Byrd stated, bringing Jamal back to reality.

Still pacing, Jamal was in deep though. This wasn't the way he meant for things to turn out; even though it happened to whom he considered the enemy, it was more the intent behind it; it was not a planned, deliberate attempt but more or less by happenstance.

What he had in mind was something which would galvanize the people and carry a longer impact. However, what was done was done; fate had brought him into this, as he had always believed he would go out in a hurl of gunfire. But this was not by his own choosing. How would he be looked upon? Would he be looked upon as a martyr for the struggle or a common criminal acting out of desperation to avoid capture? But he himself had broken no laws; would everyone know that? A lot of people on the street knew that Byrd and Blood were desperate men, with Blood wanted for murder and Byrd wanted for questioning in a double murder. Some would figure he had just gotten caught up with them. If he could somehow get to Cathy, she was a writer, and he could have her politicize this thing, but then he thought there was too much at stake; he couldn't afford to trust her in this situation. Maybe he could write something up and mail it to her; he had her address in his wallet. Yeah, he could do that, but would she do it? Well, he had nothing to lose by trying. Snake, their contact, could mail it to her.

Chapter 20

The city was in an uproar; the police departments were carrying out their vengeance on the black community. They had converged upon the house on Twenty-third where Jamal lived and tore it up, destroying everything in the process. They were doing a house-to-house search in his neighbor; they were stopping people in the middle of the street, slamming them up against cars, ransacking people's homes, putting guns to people's heads. One man resisted and was nearly beaten to death. People were being hauled in for questioning, but nobody seemed to know anything about Jamal. Nobody had hardly even seen him around the neighborhood.

Inspector Crawford, who was in charge of the case, was getting angry and frustrated for not being able to get any leads. He was just on the verge of rounding up some possible suspects in the Vinewood massacre when this "mad-dog killing," as he termed it, jumped off. Since this case superseded the massacre, he had to turn the other over to one of his subordinates, and they would get the credit for the investigative work he had done. Right now it seemed as though he hadn't a possible clue as to where these mad-dog killers may be hiding. Nobody seemed to know anything. Well, goddamnit! What kind of nigger was this they were looking for? Didn't he hang out anywhere? What were his habits? Did he do drugs? Did he sell drugs? Was he one of those . . . what they call . . . balers who like to party and spend money? Did he have a girlfriend or any friends? His name was Jamal; maybe he was a Muslim, one of those religious fanatics—that's it, it's got to be. Why didn't he think of that earlier? Who were the other two clowns? Nobody knows who they were either.

He was waiting for reports to come back. His only hope now was to see how much money the department was willing to put up for the rewards. Money always enticed these fools on the street, he reasoned. If he could get it up to two million dollars it might lead him somewhere. He would shoot for five million, and they would probably drop down to two million. He prepared himself to go in and talk to the commissioner.

"Five million dollars! Are you nuts? We can't get up that kind of money," Commissioner Adams said.

"This is no ordinary case. Those were three of our best officers, plus the female who was slain in this incident."

"Yeah I know, it's definitely high profile. Maybe *America's Most Wanted* and Detroit Clearing-House will put up a nice sum, along with the solicitation of funds for the slain officers families. Let me see what we can do," the commissioner said.

Inspector Crawford, now back in his office, was wracking his brain for a motive for the killings.

"There was no apparent motive," he wrestled with himself. Were these guys big drug dealers that panicked once they saw Bates and McLawrey, who were referred to on the streets as Smith and Wesson, noted for the quick-trigger, roughneck tactics that they employed on the city's Westside? Or were these some maniac killers, seeking revenge for some of the tactics used by Bates and McLawrey? A knock came at his door. It was Lieutenant Mason.

"Here are the reports, sir, they just arrived."

"Thank you, have a seat while I go over these." He studied them a minute then said, "I see they recovered the van?"

"Yes, the van had been stolen from the Eastside."

"Was it lifted for prints?"

"Yes, but the only prints that matched anything was the man's whose name was registered at the motel."

"Oh yeah, that Jamal Rush guy; well that tells us if the van was stolen, either these men had already done something or were planning to do something. I doubt very seriously that they would kill those policemen and that female all on account of a stolen van," the inspector theorized.

"You're right, that doesn't seem too logical, but it also doesn't seem too logical that they would kill those officers before they committed a crime either," Mason shot back.

"Good thinking, that leaves us with the conclusion that these men had already committed a crime and panicked when they spotted Bates and McLawrey."

"So what'll we do now?" Lieutenant Mason asked.

"Well, I see by this report where this Rush fellow was convicted a of armed robbery of a big supermarket that turned bad and erupted into a shootout where one of the robbers was shot and killed and a police officer was seriously wounded. So the first thing we need to do is run a check throughout the city and surrounding suburbs for any recent robberies or large thefts."

"Okay, will do," Mason said, getting up.

"Raymond, you can't go out, it's too risky. That Down River gang has people on the lookout for you," Tynetta, Raymond's girl, said.

"I've got to get in touch with my uncle; we're in the same boat."

"No, no, no, honey, his situation is a lot more severe. He's on some America's ten most wanted, public enemy number one shit; he can't even breath wrong," she said.

"Yeah, but they might not kill him."

"Are you crazy! Didn't you see the news? They told police or anybody else not to even try to arrest them because they know they're going out shooting."

"Yeah, you definitely right about that," Raymond agreed after he thought about it.

He still wanted to talk with Jamal, though, feeling that would clear his conscious somewhat as he felt responsible for his uncle's present predicament. Even though he never told his uncle to get involved directly, he knew that he would try to assist him, when in actuality all of this nonsense started happening due to his greed and desire for material comfort. He chose to stay on knowing that if it came to this Jamal would come to his aid. He also knew that his mother was blaming him for getting her brother caught up in this mess.

This constantly ate at his conscience. He would have to risk going out in order to get to the right people who could get in touch with his uncle. The only person he could think of was Li'l Al; he thought about sending Tynetta, but Li'l Al would trust no one he didn't know personally and the only reason he would be trusted was that he was Jamal's nephew. Yes, he would go out; there was no more to be said on that.

"Mr. Carrington, your daughter is out here waiting to see you. She said you sent for her," his secretary told him.

"I did; send her in."

Cathy was sitting in one of the soft chairs reading a book when the secretary came to escort her into her father's office.

"Have a seat, pudding."

"Oh Lord, I know what's coming next when you call me that."

"Well you really put me on the spot this time with Mr. London having me hire that mad-dog-killer friend of your. Mr. London will never trust my recommendations on anything from now on."

"Hold on a moment before you jump to any conclusions. We don't know if my friend is the one who actually did that," Cathy defended.

"I see, and I suppose Mr. London is going to see it that way."

"Mr. London doesn't know the man. To him all blacks are either criminals or potential criminals."

"That's not so. Where did you ever get that idea?" he said surprised.

"Well its true. He may not say it openly, but it's implied in his attitude and mannerisms when the subject of race comes up."

Mr. Carrington was embarrassed that his daughter felt like that toward his wealthy friend. She was accusing his friend of being a bigot and racist after all he had done for blacks. He had even saved a black-owned company from going out of business; of course he wound up owning the business himself years later.

"Cathy, I think you have the wrong impression of Mr. London. He has helped more blacks than the law allows."

"He has capitalized off their situation and in the process has become more wealthy," Cathy stated.

"How dare you come into this office, young lady, with those type of accusations. You've been listening to that revolutionary nut friend of yours and have allowed him to get inside of your head; I know all about your little escapades."

"You've been snooping on me?" Cathy accused.

"No not snooping, just concerned."

"You're taking that concern too far. I'm a grown woman."

"But you're still my daughter."

"You have no right to meddle in my affairs like that," she said, getting up and storming out of the office.

"Cathy, wait! Cathy! Cathy. . . ."

Inspector Crawford had finally gotten the reward up to two million dollars—enough, he figured, to entice the maybe loyal friends of these mad-dog killers. Other than that, he had nothing to work with; there were no informers, and no recent robberies of such a nature had occurred. The only thing he had to go on was what he was waiting on at the moment, which was Jamal's prison file to be located, which might perhaps provide some information as to family, relatives, and friends and associates. The trouble with locating his file was due to him being discharged rather than being on parole, which would have provided immediate access to his file. He hoped that it hadn't gotten lost in the shuffle. There was a knock at the door. *Good*, he thought, *maybe it's Mason with the reports I'm waiting on.* Instead it was the delivery boy with his lunch; he'd forgotten all about it. He ordered ham and cheese and coffee. The coffee in the station tasted terrible, maybe because he drank so much of it. Anyway, the coffee from the new deli was superb.

As he began eating his lunch there was another knock at the door. "Come in!" he growled. It was Lieutenant Mason.

"Well Goddam! It's about time.

"They had a lot of trouble locating this," he said as he tossed the file on the inspector's desk.

The inspector finished one of the sandwiches and washed it down with his coffee, wiped his hands with a napkin, and dug right into the file. After about five minutes he looked up at Mason.

"Man, this little son of a bitch is clever. He's got his family all split up and living all over the country. He's got relatives listed in about every state in the country; he has no friends or associates listed. It was like he was planning something the minute he got arrested for his last crime. The one thing I did notice, though, is that his father was killed by police during the riot and it later was discovered that he was shot while surrendering, which cost the state a helluva lawsuit."

"So what are you thinking. Inspector, motive?"

"Exactly, this guy has been carrying a grudge ever since he came into the knowledge of that."

"His mother should be a wealthy woman then?"

"She is, but according to this he hasn't lived with her since he was a teenager."

"So she probably has no idea of his whereabouts?"

"I doubt it, but we will try and locate her anyway."

"What type of work does she do?" Mason asked.

"I told you this son of a bitch is clever; he has her listed under five different job titles. I'm beginning to believe this whole file is one big lie or a deliberate attempt to confuse. He's got four other brothers and sisters, according to him, living in different states, all moved two or three times; you don't know where to begin to look for any of them. This clown has outsmarted us from the door; I'm telling you, this little punk has been planning something like this over half his life."

"Why do you say that?" Mason asked.

"Because in his file is a bunch of racial activities he's been involved with—prison riots, strikes, organizing group demonstrations, assaults on prison guards, all types of revolutionary stuff."

"He probably took after his father," Mason said.

"All right. I want you to have someone check out those addresses for any family listed in Wayne County!"

"We've already been through the house on Twenty-third; no sign of anyone living there but him."

"Okay, the best thing we could do is try to locate the mother. Once we do that, we can locate the rest of his family and relatives."

"Okay, will do, sir," Mason said and dashed out the office.

Chapter 21

Tynetta dosed off to sleep, and Raymond slipped the key out of her purse and eased out the door of her apartment. He looked around as he made his way to the Blazer—nobody was around; it was about one-thirty in the morning. He drove over to Charley's in hopes of catching Li'l Al or someone who could contact his uncle for him.

He went upstairs to holler at B-light.

"Yo Light!" he hollered.

"Yeah, who is it?"

"It's Ray."

"Goddamn, dog, you supposed to be laying low."

"Yeah I know, but this is important. I need someone to beep Li'l Al for me."

"Let me see if J-Mack is around. Hang up here. I'll be right back."

B-light came back with J-Mack. "Yo, what's up, Ray?"

"I need you to beep Li'l Al for me and see if he can come over here. Tell him it's important, something to do with my uncle."

"All right I goticha," J-Mack said as he left to go to the phone down the street.

"Yo, **Buzz**, I just got the call, that little punk is over at Charley's. Send two cars right away; he's driving a blue Blazer," Crusher said, giving the order.

"You know his uncle's going to want to retaliate," Sid said.

"Yeah, fuck him too. We got something for his ass," Crusher said deviously.

Over at Charley's J-Mack delivered the message to Raymond from Li'l Al.

"He'll be over in about fifteen minutes; he said hold tight."

Two cars pulled up across the street from Charley's.

"That's the Blazer," a deep voice said, talking to Buzz.

"Okay, we're on cue; keep your eyes open."

Five minutes later a car pulled up, and you could see a little fellow stepping out of a BMW.

"Ain't that Li'l Al?" Buzz said to the people in the back seat.

"Yeah, looks like him," the fellow with the deep voice said.

"Damn, this shit is going to turn into a full-scale war if dudes like him and his crew get involved," Buzz said.

Li'l Al went upstairs and hollered, "B-light!"

"Yo, that you, Al?"

"Yeah, coming up."

"What's going on fellas?" Li'l Al spoke to everyone in general.

"Ain't nothing, Al," everybody responded back.

"Raymond's in the back room; he wants to holler in private," B-light told Al.

Li'l Al went into the back room, where Raymond was sitting on a couch. "What's up, Li'l dog?" Li'l Al said, speaking to Raymond.

"Man, it's very important that I talk to my uncle, and I know that you're probably the only one that can arrange it."

"Yeah you got that part right, but ain't no way I can arrange a meeting between y'all."

"Why's that?" Raymond asked, surprised.

"'Cause he can't go nowhere right now, and nobody can go where he's at."

"Damn, not even his nephew."

"Naw, nobody, man. I'm under strict orders with that."

"You don't think he'll trust me?" Raymond said.

"It ain't that he don't trust you, but if don't nobody know, nobody can tell, and he ain't taking no chances with that."

"So I'm dead on that?"

"Yeah that's just the way it is, but if you want me to give him a message, I can do that."

"Just tell him I tried to get in touch with him and I'm feeling fucked up because he may be in this situation on account of me."

"All right, I'll take care of that," Li'l Al said and went down stairs.

"Yo Light, I'm finished here. I'm going back into my dugout," Raymond said.

"Yo, you got to stop poppin' up like that. This shit ain't no game."

"I hear ya," Raymond said as he went down the steps. He stepped out into the night air, looking around as he walked toward the Blazer. He never saw it coming—shots rang out from two directions, hitting him in the chest and dropping him to the ground. Three or four people, including Li'l Al, came running out into the street with guns blazing, shooting at the two cars that were racing to get out of the area.

"Did you see who it was?" Li'l Al asked.

"Naw, but I'm almost sure it was the Down River Mob," someone in the crowd said.

"Somebody wired them up."

They were putting Raymond in the Blazer and taking him to the hospital.

"He's still breathing. We got to get him to the hospital in a jurry; he might can make it," Short Dog said.

"Yeah and we don't need the feds snooping around," a voice from the crowd said.

Raymond was taken into the emergency ward and left as no one wanted to be questioned by the police when they arrived.

Jamal was looking at the news when a news brief came across the screen; *Young black male gunned down in a driveby shooting on Warren Avenue near the Jefferson Freeway. He is listed in critical condition.*

"Yo Byrd, you hear that?"

"Naw, what's up?"

"Somebody was gunned down right by Charley's."

"Y.K.2. huh?"

"Probably so."

"I know what you thinking," Byrd said.

Right then Blood came from upstairs. They were living in a fallout shelter built by rich white folks after the attack on Pearl Harbor.

"Li'l Al's on his way over," Blood said.

"All right, make sure he's by himself, then buzz him in," Byrd said.

Jamal was thinking what he would do if that was his nephew who was gunned down. He certainly would be taking a heck of a risk by going out, but at the same time he definitely couldn't let them get away with harming someone in his family. But hadn't Raymond somewhat brought that on himself, if it was him, he wrestled with himself—and if it was him, would it be worth risking everything now just to avenge him? As he was thinking, he heard the trap door open; he saw Byrd up checking things out as Li'l Al and Blood came down the trap steps.

"Damn, Byrd, you got a helluva hookup here."

"Yeah, yeah, I ain't going to make it easy for nobody to get me."

"Yeah I see," Li'l Al said.

"What brings you over here at this time?" Jamal asked Li'l Al.

"Your nephew."

Jamal's heart skipped a beat. "That was him, huh?"

"Damn how you know that?"

"It was on the news already."

"Man, you ain't going to believe this. He had just sent for me to try and arrange a meeting between you and him, and after I told him it wasn't possible, he told me to tell you that he felt responsible for what happened in your situation and as soon as he left and stepped out the door is when they opened up on him."

"Well how did they know he was coming out or when he was coming out?"

"Somebody tipped them off."

"Damn fool suppose to had stayed put," Jamal said angrily.

"Wasn't he staying with some chick?" Byrd asked.

"Supposed to been," Li'l Al said.

Jamal was thinking quietly for a moment when Byrd blurted out. "So whats's up now?"

"What's up now! Them clowns got to go that's what up." Jamal's whole character seemed to change. Everyone knew he was ready to make a move and couldn't be stopped.

"Well this is what started it; I guess this what's going to finish it," Blood said, and the room fell silent.

They had all heard the news; by now Raymond had been identified, and was in the intensive care unit and not expected to make it.

"This family's just falling apart. I told you a long time ago you should move out of that neighborhood," Yolanda's mother told her.

"Mama, it's not the neighborhood; it's the lifestyle. That boy has been attracted to that lifestyle since he was eleven years old, and they all come up now thinking that's the way to make it."

"Well, what about your brother?"

"He's different. He's got a grudge against the system, and he won't have nothing to do with no drugs or anything else that will harm his people," Yolanda said being very articulate in drawing the distinction between her brother and her son.

"Mama, when we going to see Raymond?" Red asked.

"In a minute, soon as I get everybody ready."

"The boy might be dead by then."

"Mama, please!" Yolanda hollered at her.

"I can't believe that much tragedy can happen to one family all around the same time," Jean told Cathy as they sat on the couch watching the news.

"Yes, that's very unfortunate for the family. I can imagine the stress it's putting his sister through, having a son and a brother being gunned down like her father had been."

"Gee, I didn't know the father had been gunned down, too."

"He was killed by the police during the '67 riots."

"Blacks really do have it rough, don't they?" Jean commented.

"Yes, they really do; it's a struggle as soon as they come into this world," Cathy said, thinking of Jamal.

"It would seem as though after all these years things would have changed for them."

"The only change that has been made is that society is doing a better job in covering it up," Cathy said, again catching herself answering in the manner of Jamal.

"You could write a story just on their lives alone: The father killed by the police, the son goes to prison, gets out, and is now on the ten most wanted list, the nephew gunned down in the street at the same time his uncle is being hunted—quite a story," Jean said.

"You're absolutely correct, an action-packed story. Have you ever thought how different their lives are from ours? Their lives are filled with drama, never a dull moment, high risk day to day," Cathy said, her mind wandering.

"As opposed to our dull, go-to-school, go-to-work, come-home, look-at-T.V., study, go-to-bed, no-real-adventures life," Jean commented.

"And the killing part is that their lives are filled with this adventure just from trying to survive."

Yolanda and her family were in the emergency room waiting and were not allowed in the intensive care unit where Raymond was being operated on.

"Mama, why we can't see Raymond?" Poochi asked.

"Look boy, you heard that man say we can't go in there while they're operating on him."

"What if he die?"

"There's nothing we can do if that happens."

"I want to see my brother before he die."

"Shut up, Red. Nobody said he gon' die," Wanda told her.

The police were there to try to question him but were not allowed in the intensive care unit either. They had no idea that this was the family of Jamal. Raymond and Jamal had different last names, so no one was able to make the connection, and of course, no one volunteered.

The family waited for hours, praying and hoping that Raymond would survive this. If he did, the family reasoned, it may turn his whole life around. The top surgeon working on Raymond came out of the intensive care unit, pulling off his surgical mask with a tired and frustrated look on his face as he approached Yolanda.

"We tried all we could, Mrs. Townsend."

"I understand," she said softly with tears building up in the corners of her eyes as she tried to remain strong.

"He dead, huh Mama?" Poochi said.

"Yes, he's at peace now. Let's all go home."

"You mean to tell me that all this time nobody figured out that the young boy that was gunned down on Warren and the expressway was the nephew of the man we're looking for?" Inspector Crawford told Lieutenant Mason.

"Well nobody was able to make the connection at first as they don't have the same last name."

"What about the goddamn address? According to this," he was looking at the report in his hand, "the nephew's address is listed as the same address that was raided looking for the murder suspect in the police killings."

"Correct, sir, but he had two other addresses listed also, which caused a mix-up."

"Okay, we'll get back to that. Has anyone in that family been contacted and questioned yet?"

"We're in the process of doing that now, sir."

"What the hell kind of clowns you got working on this, Mason?"

"That couldn't be helped, sir. There was no one at the residence when my officers went out there."

"Well you better hope to hell someone shows up fast or you're going to find yourself off this case."

"Yes sir, will that be all?"

"Yeah, get the hell outta here."

Chapter 22

Jamal had just finished packing his explosives. To him the move was worth the risk. He had gotten word that his nephew had died as a result of the gunshot wounds. There was nothing else to discuss, nothing else to contemplate; his mind was made up; they would move tonight.

Byrd and Blood were busy cleaning and loading their guns. They understood the high risk that was involved. To them, the end of the rope had come once they shot those police officers; in the back of their minds they did not see themselves coming out from under this alive. They accepted their fate and were ready to take it the whole nine yards.

Cathy had received the letter from Jamal explaining his plight to gain her support and rally to his defense. He told her that the police had been planning to assassinate him from the moment he had been released from the riot incident and that they had done a background check on him and found out that he recently had been released from prison for shooting a policeman. He was supposedly holding a grudge against the police department for killing his father and was assumed to be planning some retaliatory action against them.

They discovered that he had rented a room at the Cadillac Motel and noticed some suspicious characters visiting him. He believed they were planning a sneak attack upon him at the motel.

He told her he had gotten a tip from someone who knew someone who worked in the department, that they would be coming for him. So when he spotted the officers in the parking lot checking out his car, he assumed that they were coming for him. When he and his friends decided to leave the room they met the officers on the steps, and the officers reached for their guns; that's when all hell broke loose. The female, he assumed, got caught in the crossfire as the officer in the squad car reached for his gun.

He emphasized that no matter what the outcome was of all this, that's the version she must tell. After reading the letter she concluded that she would go to bat for him as she believed he was targeted by the police department, regardless of how she felt about his version.

Inspector Crawford was sitting behind his desk going through some files when a hard knock came at his door. He looked up from the files and hollered out in anger. Come in before you knock the damn door down.

"Goddamnit, Mason, you better have something," the inspector growled at him.

"I just got a hot tip," Mason said with urgency in his voice.

"I hope this is reliable and not another one of those crackpots."

"Well, it's a long shot, but I think you might want to ride with this one."

"Okay, Mason, let me have it."

"Well, now that we know that the boy who was killed on Warren Avenue is the nephew of the suspect in the police murders, we have found out that the uncle is planning a retaliation move against the Down River Mob, who he feels was responsible for his nephew's murder."

"Okay, now what?"

"Well the tip is that the uncle and his crew have targeted the house on the boulevard down by the riverfront."

"How did you get that information?" Inspector Crawford asked with suspicion.

"They were spotted casing out the house of the top distributors of the Mob."

"Well what the hell are you waiting for? Get a stakeout out there right away."

"Will do, sir."

"That's the house," Jamal told Byrd as he drove around the block. Byrd parked the car a couple of housed away.

"That's them," Lieutenant Mason, who was in a van parked across the street, said to Detective Gilmore, who had tactical command of the operation.

"All right, call for backup; we move when they move," Gilmore said.

Jamal told Byrd and Blood to get ready. They stepped out of the car and ducked down with their sights set on the house. Jamal jumped out of the car and ran up to the house and tossed the bomb (which he put together) through the front window.

BOOM! A big explosion erupted.

"What the hell was that!" Lieutenant Mason said with shock.

"Okay, let's move out," Detective Gilmore said. They all jumped out of the van with guns drawn, running toward the car.

"Police! Put your weapons down!"

Blood and Byrd rolled over on the ground at the same time and started shooting immediately, hitting one of the officers. The return of gunfire was overwhelming yet missed Byrd and Blood due to their position on the ground.

Jamal lit two sticks of dynamite and threw them in the direction of the police. By now the entire block was filled with law enforcement. Helicopters flew above them.

Some of the people who were in that house came running out, and Jamal was able to pick off one or two of them. The whole scene turned into a war zone, with Byrd and Blood still firing their automatic weapons. All of a sudden a big flash of light fell from above, landing directly in front of the car where Byrd and Blood were shielding themselves and causing an explosion which killed both Byrd and Blood.

The only thing that saved Jamal was that he had strayed toward the house trying to catch Crusher and some of his crew coming out. When it was all over he lay wounded on the sidewalk after catching bullets in his shoulder, leg, and side. He was placed into custody by Detroit police and taken to Detroit General Hospital in an ambulance and treated for gunshot wounds while still heavily guarded. T.V. cameras were everywhere. The press were anxious to get a story.

Cathy rushed to the hospital once she found out about the incident. She had gotten a press card from one of her father's friends. She had finally made it to his room, but before entering she had to go through a metal detector just as anyone else who entered did. She found him strapped to the bed in what appeared to be a straightjacket. He looked up and saw her and said to himself, *Damn, I didn't want her to see me like this.*

She always seemed to show up at an awkward time. How the hell did she get in there anyway?

She came closer to the bed and whispered, "Looks as though you may not make it to work after all," she said with a smile.

"Yeah, probably not," he said also with a smile, then added, "Did you get my letter?"

Yes, and I'll let that be known. But how did you get yourself caught up in this fix?"

"I don't know. Some things you don't see coming, and when you realize what's up, it's too late—you're already caught up in it. It's like an invisible web. . . ."